A GOLD SHEAF ON A GREY THRONE

DRAGAN BALOG

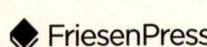 FriesenPress

Suite 300 - 990 Fort St
Victoria, BC, V8V 3K2
Canada

www.friesenpress.com

Copyright © 2017 by Dragan (Ed) Balog
First Edition — 2017

All rights reserved.

No part of this publication may be reproduced in any form, or by any means, electronic or mechanical, including photocopying, recording, or any information browsing, storage, or retrieval system, without permission in writing from FriesenPress.

ISBN
978-1-5255-0845-5 (Hardcover)
978-1-5255-0846-2 (Paperback)
978-1-5255-0847-9 (eBook)

1. FICTION, SMALL TOWN & RURAL

Distributed to the trade by The Ingram Book Company

THIS BOOK IS DEDICATED TO:

My children: son **Mihajlo** and daughter **Maja** - within each of us there is a creative force. Always aspire to achieve the highest levels in whatever you do. Believe in yourselves, dream big and never ever give up -
hard work always pays off.

ACKNOWLEDGEMENTS

I will be forever thankful to my wife - Nedjeljka, family and numerous friends, who have given me the courage, inspiration and strength to complete my new book.

PREFACE

A Gold Sheaf On A Grey Throne is based on a resource-rich fictional town - Bagerville, which at the behest of the nation's government leases everything in its higher elevations area to a powerful foreign economic entity. As a result, reduced sovereignty and the operation of an autonomous and special economic and customs zone are created, while many legislations and regulations are also altered.

During the transition of this once sleepy town into an industrial mecca, many become disgusted at the shackle of corrupt power structures destroying the town's rich historical past, and decide to seek ways to bring about more transparency and accountability to the activities.

Arrogance, corruption, dissent, greed, intrigue, narcissism and redemption are at the heart of the battle, when the political, legal and economic systems are amended through duress and monetary compensation after a major global economic downturn.

Throughout history with power comes great responsibility, though with absolute power corruption always rears its ugly head and begins to infect humanities mind and soul, as is the case in *A Gold Sheaf On A Grey Throne*.

Dragan (Ed) Balog

TABLE OF CONTENTS

Acknowledgements	III
Preface	V
Chapter 1—Bagerville	1
Chapter 2—ViGnChi meeting at The Intra	14
Chapter 3—The Sundial	23
Chapter 4—A Parting of Ways	33
Chapter 5—The Data Breach	41
Chapter 6—Teach and Meet	47
Chapter 7—Solace	57
Chapter 8—Opposite Directions	64
Chapter 9—Jason at The Polytechnic	69
Chapter 10—The Art of Deception	79
Chapter 11—Found	86
Chapter 12—Recovery	92
Chapter 13—A War of Words	96
Chapter 14—Q90	107
Chapter 15—GN-MG HQ	113
Chapter 16—Who, What, Where, Why, When?	119
Chapter 17—Researching for the Truth	123
Chapter 18—The Final Act of Redemption	129

CHAPTER 1
BAGERVILLE

Overlooking a small ravine across an autumn landscape, Bagerville Polytechnic Geologist and Professor Jason Dallas sat in his chair next to his desk, paging through some results in his cozy two-storey house, just a kilometre away from the centre of town. After university he returned to his hometown and took up a teaching position at the now renowned Bagerville Polytechnic, in an area he knew every inch of the territory - and every granule of sand, seed and water composites by heart.

Above in the distance of the haunting higher elevations, the resource-rich mountainous areas, above the Soma River, were known as the Q90 area, where smouldering plumes of dark pollution were emitting a new industrial frequency and reality, welcomed by many and hated by a few. Bagerville was home to some haunting landscapes, where the mountains and all under them were found to contain vast sums of minerals and base metals, which the government quickly leased, as a special economic zone, to a consortium, after a catastrophic global economic downturn. Adding strength to the deal was Mayor Joe Bohlm, who was then a tad more visible, and a lot more vocal on all municipal issues, frequently stating, "Better days are ahead of us. There are tremendous opportunities coming to Bagerville soon. Very soon the world will finally see Bagerville as an economic powerhouse."

During the turmoil, the nation's president, John E. Lornae, in his second four-year term, began to aggressively attend many international conferences, summits and meetings of political and business leaders. During one of those events, he met behind closed doors with the

ViGnChi consortium, who presented an idea to him, which immediately caught his ears. He had his legal teams look through the proposal, and some in his inner cabinet remembered Lornae's words, "First, this has to be pitched as a motion, before being brought to light to the various levels of government. This document will also require major consensus and consultation, before any legal frameworks can begin. Then my signature in Ophidia and Bagerville's will be needed. We're also going to have to expropriate a lot of land in Bagerville for the developments and infrastructure needed. It may cause a few ruffled feathers with the folks down there."

Another major project over a hundred plus kilometres further away was the untapped Epsilon 4 area, where there were rumours from some researchers of vast deposits of many different ores, though due to the lack of roads and small indigenous communities that resided there, exploration was still decades away.

Bagerville quickly transformed into an engine of growth, after the government altered legislation and regulations to satisfy ViGnChi, that in essence bailed the nation out of one of the world's worst economic downturns. The ViGnChi plan accelerated quickly, and within a few years, the Q90 area of Bagerville was humming to the ubiquitous sounds of: mining, manufacturing, refining and precision detailing of highly intricate components. Within a short time span, it changed this once sleepy arable and fertile area, and helped to employ thousands of people from all points of the globe and the nation, in its various kaleidoscope of economic entities. During the transition many of Bagerville's core businesses in agriculture and viticulture, quickly became a thing of the past, as many were forced to sell their lands under duress, due to the march of progress.

Furthering to the boom was the massive infrastructure spending and transition of the region's small Bagerville airport, situated a few kilometres from the centre. Once used by small planes and helicopters, now it got new runway extensions, new control tower, customs office and expanded airport terminal. This expansion proved beneficial, as Ophidia got four new daily flights to Bagerville, in both directions, with travel time being just over thirty-five minutes. Adding to the expansion were new increased domestic and international flights a few times weekly, all within the nearby Q90 - which were reachable by new roads, new rail-line and spur. As a result, many valuable Bagerville properties, businesses and lands continued to vanish, while some were expropriated at an alarming rate, causing more angst with many Bagerville townsfolk.

The academic, business, scientific and engineering communities experienced a boom as well, particularly the Bagerville Polytechnic where many cheered the booming economy and enrolments. Further, most large projects, required microscopic insights on many social, economic and environmental issues, as this area became a huge cash cow for some coffers. With the wild expansion, there were a few major bones of contention: reduced sovereignty and highly probable corruption. Some of the talk in the town was, "There are tentacles and invisible hands, hiding under the cloak of secrecy, breeding corruption and evil seeds in the minds of our townsfolk." Monetary compensation always made its way into the pockets of those that could influence the levers of power. Bagerville's Mayor Joe Bohlm was one with influence, and always looked for a cut, since rumours circulated that he often reminded some business leaders, "All deals are possible behind closed doors for a smile, handshake, wink and an envelope."

The forces of change also created the demise of the once annual Bagerville Harvest fair, held each autumn. It was a well-known national fair, with Bagerville's famous Ferris wheel, rides and a stage where bands played. The stage also had a great sound system, where speakers could go up and talk about various issues. Further, vendor booths were always set up, where merchants could sell produce and other goods. In addition, there was even an annual exhibit by the town's geology professor, who showcased Bagerville and Q90's abundant resources of Titanium, Palladium and Tungsten. Since the ViGnChi consortium set-up operations, some of Bagerville's last remaining farms, which for a few generations grew corn and wheat, or apple or cherry orchards, all slowly began to go out of business or sell their lands. Bagerville saw a forced reduction in agricultural interest, once the higher paying mining and manufacturing jobs took root, with many reluctantly flocking away from their ancestral pastures to the lucrative ones of ViGnChi.

The Bagerville viticulture industry was also reduced to just two now - the Jensson Wineries and the Valddem Estates. It was the town's native son and Mayor Joe Bohlm, who also scrapped the annual Bagerville Harvest Fair a few years back citing, "Changing demographics and market conditions." Deeply offended by everything unfolding, Geologist and Professor Jason Dallas, who would often rail and decry the changes in his native Bagerville. Jason Dallas often stated, "The Bagerville Harvest Fair was about our deep historic roots in this town - a cultural element that defines us. It brought in many people from all points, bringing tourists to town was also economical beneficial to local businesses. The fair was not just nostalgic, but a bridge builder from the past and into the future."

Jason was there at one of those first secretive meetings at The Intra Hotel, many years ago and never concealed his distaste for everything that was unfolding before his eyes. But his disgust for Q90, was nowhere in comparison to some individuals in Bagerville, who lusted for dark deals. Yet with the protests that he began, he quickly learned that there were still many in town that shared his visions, and were also against the new changes taking hold of their town. In Ophidia, President Lornae rose in parliament during those changing hours and reminded everyone, "Should we sink into the depths of a dark economic abyss, you will be judged by the people, for failing to prevent something we had the power to prevent." Some parliamentarians were not only fearful for their political seats, but also of the new reality that was unfolding, and many whispered in quiet corners, "We fear Lornae will strong-arm the opposition in parliament to acquiesce to radical legislative and regulatory changes through fear."

The metamorphosis of Bagerville poisoned the air of tranquility, as the opposing voices grew against the new reality, and vowed to resist its chains of domination and subjugation of the town's spirit. Professor Jason Dallas, along with some of those voices, became more active and emboldened to resist unethical conduct, questionable policies and corruption, thus spearheading more frequent town protests, some of which made international headlines. "The soul of Bagerville is not for sale. Don't destroy everything that was built over generations," Jason could be heard shouting near Mayor Bohlm's office, with what started with a half dozen protesters with placards, many times since word broke of ViGnChi coming to develop the Q90 area a few years ago. During one of the protests, Joe Bohlm came out of his office, approaching Jason Dallas, before diplomatically relaying a clear message, "Jason, there are higher powers that have decided upon this. Our old friend from South Eastern, Minister Milton Ferron, called me. He told me about Lornae's decision. It isn't perfect, but look at the way the globe is spinning these days. The downturn is real. It was only a matter of time, before we felt something here. That said, the decision would make Bagerville richer, create more opportunities for our communities, and help pay for more services and infrastructure that we need. Jason, I know you love Bagerville. I loved your grandpa Jim Dallas too. He was like a father figure many times to all of us growing up. I remember the good times we had. Being out in the fields, the fishing, the bike rides, the Bagerville Fair, but his is now. This is a new reality. The world has changed. I love this place, with all my heart, but this will give Bagerville what it needs for the next one hundred years."

Jason just stood straight up, lowered his placard, and unapologetically retorted back to Bohlm with a cold stare, "How could you agree to this? How could you sign those documents in our name? Have you lost your ethical and moral compass? One consortium? How could you? Since we were kids, me, you, Ruddy and Frank vowed that we would remain here, protect our way of life. We all vowed to protect the Soma, the agriculture, the vineyards and the higher elevations from exploitation amongst other things. Now the Moltracheen Estates, next the Voss and Zelk fields will be on your radar for expropriation. Also, I noticed you have amended the zoning laws for new industrial, commercial and residential areas. You are giving away permits for new developments that are going to overshadow the skyline of Bagerville. Why? Peaceful and non-violent resistance will be the rallying call. These protests will continue!"

Jason then raised his placard once again, before shouting, "Shame on you, Joe! Bagerville is not for sale!"

At that point, a sombre Mayor Joe Bohlm turned his back, and slowly walked back to his offices, closing the door, before letting out a big exhale. Jason's words sent a chill up his spine, but his convictions and desires were still geared towards a new dawn for Bagerville and his personal fortunes.

It wasn't too long ago that Bohlm had finished with a meeting in his office with some local residents and staff that he sat down at his desk, and looked at his call display on his phone that rang. The Ministry of Economic Affairs number from the nation's capital Ophidia lit up on his rectangular view screen. Bohlm just kept looking at the phone, as it rang twice, before answering, "Mayor Bohlm?"

"Mr. Joe Bohlm? Mayor Joe Bohlm," a very familiar voice began.

"Milt? Milton Ferron, Minister of Economic Affairs. How the heck are you old pal? Still using everything Sula taught us at South Eastern?" asked a now more jovial Bohlm.

"He's now running Bagerville Polytechnic, and Dallas is teaching there too?" Ferron quickly asked.

"Yes sir. So, I've heard some rumours coming out of Ophidia. I heard something about Bagerville. Lornae has been in the news quite a bit in the past few weeks. Something in the pipes?" Bohlm began quizzing his old friend from his university days.

Ferron calmly took a deep breath before beginning, "Some tough decisions and proposals are being examined at many levels. Before the wind carries the stories, you need to know about it. Lornae and a consortium - ViGnChi - have been having some very high-level talks. We're looking at amending some key legislations and regulations to enable this. Parliament is seething. The opposition is furious that we're attempting to bypass them. Drastic measures need to be taken. They're eying Bagerville's vast resources at Q90. They would like to have a special economic zone for the area under the ViGnChi umbrella. Ophidia will try to get your signature on the deal. Short term pain for long-term gain."

Bohlm listened with more enthusiasm than scepticism, and simply answered back, "What's in it for me Milt? What do I get in return? There are some here in Bagerville that may resist this fiercely - Dallas and Sark to name but a few."

Ferron paused for a moment, before continuing, "I need you to keep this under wraps for now. I trust you. I'm just a messenger. Lornae doesn't know about my call to you yet. Joe, your signature will be crucial for this deal. We'll get into the finer details at another date. Not over the phone. Too many eyes and ears. We're looking at The Intra for the event. Titanium, Palladium and Tungsten are prized possessions. The appetite is enormous, and the price tag is equally important for Ophidia. It may be a sacrifice, but many feel that Epsilon 4 is still years away from exploring."

Joe Bohlm continued listening before he once again asked, "What do I get in return Milt?"

Ferron once again took a deep breath and countered back, "You'll meet with the ViGnChi consortium people - Vilmajev, Chiu and Gunthar of ViGnChi - soon. Mr. Gunthar will be your most important point man to deal with. I'm sure the two of you will get along. Let's just say that they may have some lucrative mechanisms available to enhance your active and growing lifestyle."

The chain of events forever changed the nation and Bagerville a few years ago. For Jason Dallas though, he was one of the town's greatest patriots. Those changing events played in his mind like a newsreel, which he wished he could erase at any cost. Yet every time he looked out of his windows, the nostalgic images of Bagerville were replaced by the new realities. Shaking his salt and pepper hair, and looking back to his computer monitor, he peaked out of his window again to a new angle, towards two empty grey barns, silos and combines parked next to them – symbols of a great past, which caused him to pause, reflect and sigh.

For a moment, he glanced away from the distractions to one of the top shelves in his study room, where he kept his small rock samples with their atomic numbers and names. On the next shelf were some of his older tools - a chisel, crack hammer, compass and his first hand lens magnifier. Another of his prized instruments was at one corner his large desk - his Petrographic microscope - which he used for rock imaging and analysis. He performed many "Pols" or PLMs known as polarized light microscopy with this valuable instrument on the finds from Q90. He analyzed many of the metallic ores, after he cut them thinly, lapping and polishing and sometimes even grinding the material down to view their properties at ten microns on a slide.

His focus shifted once again to the rocks. The one that stood out the most was the silver-grey, light alloy that usually melts over the 1600-Celsius mark - Titanium. The higher elevations of Bagerville had enormous quantities of it in the mines, in addition to Palladium, Tungsten and other ores.

Over the past few years, the value per ounce for most of those alloys on many global bourse and exchanges shot up to historic levels. He remembered many times going up into the Q90, hundreds of feet underground examining the hidden terrain of veins, to confirm the many topographic maps and GPS surveys he examined, with many people. The contours, lines, depressions and the many valuable veins at different depths, where his camera took countless snapshots, some used by many resource libraries, educational and government institutes globally. His hand lens and crack hammer had lots of work in the Q90, so he was well versed. Those pictures were captured in many photo albums and disks in his study and office at Bagerville Polytechnic still.

As his peripheral vision was blurring, he remembered as a child walking past a convenience store nestled near a corner, where bushels of grapes and apples were sitting under a large overhead sign. Many elegant and smartly dressed couples were walking near the sidewalks smiling at their infants in strollers. He took an emotional deep breath, before reflecting on a time when glorious gold fields of wheat and green cornstalks were the focal point from any distance. He stopped, took another deep breath and focused on the present again.

As he twitched his shoulder, he noticed a single grey strand of hair descending from his scalp in an epic fashion - beginning an effortless and forlorn fall, where it meshed like a chameleon on the grainy hardwood floors. He glanced at the strand of grey hair, before noticing a family photo album on one of his shelves. Many family photos and memories, some of him, Gordana and Matt, from the formative years to the past year. How time flew. The wild horses had run away from the stables, and so too did his youth, as once again he looked at the grey strand that reminded him of how short life is.

It was still early, as he glanced above at the ornate clock above the doorway now, which had both hands pointing in opposite directions

- 6:50 AM. He smirked, and realized, "a coffee or tea now is not only desirable, but of utmost importance, before I can continue." Without causing a ruckus in the house, he quickly made a four-cup fix in his percolating unit that he had been making, in the room and poured himself a mug.

From another room, within seconds, drum-like patterns raced down the stairs yelling, "Morning." Matt was almost in the kitchen, before a small hailstorm of shoe polish canisters and no less than three individual shoes lying on a top step tumbled down the stairs after him.

Catching a deep breath, after the almost aerobic jaunt from upstairs, his eyes became momentarily fixated at the TV, where another story about Q90, Bagerville and ViGnChi was being mentioned. The story began narrating some facts about the town's transition from primarily agricultural simplicity, to future significance, as a result of vast wealth of resources in the higher elevations. The entrepreneurs behind the Q90 initiative were - Boris Vilmajev, Thomar Gunthar and Yan Chiu.

Global giant, ViGnChi was known for their extensive contract work with: precision instruments, medical, automotive, aerospace, aviation and the military industries, employing tens of thousands of people on many continents. Within a short time frame, some reports were coming out that - Thomar Gunthar was already indicating, "I have a desire to breakaway and launch a separate entity, in the advanced manufacturing fields of defence and aerospace."

The documentary also revealed that Bagerville Polytechnic had benefited, "From investments, bursaries, scholarships and employment opportunities for graduates of multi-disciplines." Another central theme that the documentary highlighted was, "The Gross Domestic Product (GDP) in our nation is finally inching upwards. Bagerville's economic boom has been fuelled by ViGnChi's tremendous investments in mining, new plants, manufacturing and exports, which has kick-started many cylinders of the nation's economy forward." The only concern near the end of the documentary was, "With the potential of Gunthar leaving ViGnChi, the successor rights need to be taken into account. Further, one has to speculate the nature of his new start-up in the horizon, and hope that any structural changes will have minimal job loses in Bagerville."

Matt just shrugged his head while standing there fixated to the story, knowing full well that it forever changed his town and his father, Jason Dallas, who wasn't a fan of ViGnChi or Gunthar, or any incarnations of theirs, since they landed on these shores and held their big event at The Intra Hotel years ago.

The story kept going on for about another five minutes, while Matt just stood there almost in a daze, analyzing the documentary, while in the back of his mind he wished for Q90 to be a bigger source of pride for the nation, rather than being another government giveaway to the lowest bidder.

At this point, Matt grabbed the remote control from the kitchen table, changed the channel to the weather station, and passed the puffer that had fallen on the floor to his mother.

"Looks like some rain is in the forecast. Again," sighed his mother, Gordana, as she was trying to figure out why he was in a hurry, and wouldn't stick around for breakfast.

Quickly grabbing his jacket, keys to the jeep, two slices of bacon, and a quick sip of tea from his mother's mug, he then scurried for the door with laptop and knapsack slung around his right shoulder, now jerking increments at the door knob with his right hand.

"You call that breakfast and good morning, Matt? Why don't you stay a few more minutes?' asked his mother, who was looking at him now with a slightly perturbed snare. "Well, I guess it's off to the races again," she finally changed the directional tone, before taking a few inhales from her puffer again.

"I have a few errands, and a very important computer lab to work on. I'll be back soon," he yelped back, while in the back of his mind was the documentary on Bagerville. Matt now slowly squeaked the door open again, moseyed on through, before he quickly and firmly closed it shut. He headed across the porch and down the steps into the garage, while the documentary was still on his mind, until he began humming something he heard as a kid, which made him finally laugh. He quickly hoped into his black jeep, with cap on, adjusting the rear view mirror and snapping on his seatbelt. All fired up now with adrenaline, he grabbed the keys from his pocket and doubled up on making sure his cell, knapsack and laptop were in the rear seats, before he turned on the ignition and finally drove away.

Gordana Dallas nee Torba was once a teacher, before coming down with a respiratory illness, most likely caused by exposure to silica dust particles during a fire just over two decades ago. It was Jason, who rescued her from the flames. That was the first time they met. As a child, she came to Bagerville, from one of great cities near the Danube, west of the Carpathian basin.

Back upstairs, Jason Dallas was now analyzing some charts and documents relating to the Titanium, Palladium, Tungsten and other ore deposits up in the Q90 area, when his index finger caught on a thin wood sliver on his oval shaped desk, pushing his thumb in the opposite direction, knocking over a mug of steaming black coffee over his left thigh. He always started his mornings with a coffee first, and tea after. Immediately after the spill and the finger jab, dark waters began to spread, and a few droplets of blood sprinkled over the pages he had been analyzing. He cursed the periodic table, and any acronym relating to: 22Ti, 46Pd and 74W. The pain was searing, as the fluid and heat hit an already tender spot, near his left knee.

Emotional outbursts of some well known profanities continued, echoing through the entire home and down the stairs, where Gordana could hear him crystal clear and, louder than their neighbour's dog. Gordana began laughing, and then she called out, "Jason, how about something to sooth things over?" as the teapot began to boil, for the two waiting cups of peppermint tea with lemon wedges sitting on the table.

Adding to the kitchen beauty was a small candlelight, resting in a tin casing that flickered and warmed a soap stone oil burner, holding a few droplets of sandalwood essence. The mist and aroma filled the house, and blended perfectly with the tea, creating a warm, pleasant and memory awakening spirit.

Realizing enough was enough, Jason decided to finally tidy things up. First, he decided to put the documents and charts to dry on the desk. After completing things, realizing his hands were a tad dirty, he decided to the washroom to cleanup, before finally heading downstairs for a tea. As he arrived in the kitchen, he gave his wife a kiss and sat down to chat.

He looked up at the calendar on the wall, and an approaching autumn date - it was a day that would remain forever etched in his memory.

That date was eighty-five days before New Years Eve - October 4th - vivid as if it was today, even though it happened a few years ago. He remembered looking at wristwatch and 1:30 PM, before his life changed again, and he had to rush Gordana to the hospital. She suffered a serious breathing attack, so he took her in his car to the urgent care division immediately.

Since that episode, his thoughts often drifted into the past and present, though he would always reminisce about countless smiles that pierced through the searing sun, to the many mid-day adventures and the slow dances into the sunset, that they shared together. The fall from grace, when Gordana's health began to deteriorate happened suddenly, and took its toll on the family. From dream-like state to the conscious one, Jason remembered his foot pressing harder on the accelerator as his emotions raced, with Gordana in pain, and the hospital only minutes away.

He tore down the main road doing a couple of serious digits over the limit. Tire smoke and loads of dust went flying forty-five degrees to both sides. Jason's foot pounded the accelerator past the fluorescent orange construction pylons and idle yellow backhoe and past the gravel-laid section on River Trail Road.

To the side of the road was Sheriff Ruddy of Division 01, sitting in a cruiser, sunglasses covering his tired eyes and drinking a pop. He was trying to monitor the surroundings, when Jason jetted past him. He must have been tearing thirty kilometres or more over the speed limit, before Ruddy shook his head, cussed a profanity and started to follow right behind him with his lights flashing. Ruddy pulled him over quick, now realized it was an old friend after seeing the license plate. He quickly approached the car, took his cap off, before resting his left palm on the outer edges of the rolled down car window, less than a foot from Jason. Unenthused, he looked at Jason sternly and asked him, "What's going on? You were passing at least thirty over the mark."

Jason was only mildly calm, and Ruddy sensed a problem immediately, before his response, "Ruddy. Gordana's having a breathing attack,

I'm rushing her to the hospital." He quickly turned his head to the back, to see Gordana sprawled on the back seats sweating and coughing. He looked at Ruddy now with swollen eyes and begged the question, "I don't know what's going to happen."

Seeing Gordana's condition made the still brown haired, two-hundred pound, six-footer Ruddy, begin sprinting back to his cruiser, cap flying and shouting, "Jay, follow me I'll fire up the light show and get us there quicker."

Within two minutes, they arrived at - the Bagerville General Hospital. Jason remembered seeing: the emergency ward, a stretcher, oxygen and hearing a doctor's blurred speech. Those fast paced moments flickered like a newsreel, on an old film projector in his head. From that day forward, he was constantly drifting into memories, only Gordana's voice reminding him in the kitchen, "Jason, are you there? Drink your tea," woke him from his reminiscing of the past again.

CHAPTER 2
VIGNCHI MEETING AT THE INTRA

The global downturn caused the nation's economy to spiral out of control with high unemployment, unstable price-levels and inflation. At the request of President John E. Lornae and the legal granting from Supreme Judge Bollxop, Defence Minister General William Vysten unleashed the police and military out of their bases multiple times to quell the unrest, after the Crisis Measures Protocol was enacted. The Protocol, allowed for, "Increased police and military assistance and presence, where needed, until civilian control is restored." It was mostly utilized in times of emergencies and crisis situations, where economic, political or social issues disturbed the fabric of the nation to the point that the security of the country was at risk. Thankfully in Bagerville, the nation's ire was not felt, as it was a small community then, which had a few core businesses, a Polytechnic and a robust agriculture and viticulture industry that employed many people.

As the Bagerville townsfolk were watching the events unfold, some within town were aghast when they heard of a possible 99-year lease-like deal, creating a special economic and autonomous customs zone for Q90 and the entire Bagerville-area, by a cash-strapped central government. Long time and multi-generational native and professor at Bagerville Polytechnic Jason Dallas promised many politicians, "I along with many, will be against an autonomous status for Q90 and Bagerville, especially if it is to be run, like a kingdom by one organization." Further Jason's words, "I will defend Bagerville to my last breath, if I have to," almost grew to a rallying call that quietly grew with more and more people in town. Many Bagerville townsfolk began to come out to his weekly protests, and the numbers kept growing. Some wore disguises and masks to avoid being seen, some bandanas, and many others just said, "I am here, because my voice has to be heard. I am here to protest, because I am against the encroachment on our way of life in Bagerville." One of the only people excited at the changes was mayor Bohlm, who anxiously anticipated any development that would enrich the town, though some felt that his words were more about him getting his pockets continually lined with financial resources.

But it wasn't long before the politicians exhausted all textbook theories to remedy the crisis, while depleting financial reserves to the point of having to take enormous international loans to restructure. The additional funds that were received, quickly evaporated without results, plunging the nation further into debt. The nation needed some strong medicine from the pneumonia it was trying to cure.

The national government buckled and caved in to the most unthinkable, effectively reducing their sovereignty in the Bagerville area, which was rich with resources, to a foreign economic entity, for a massive bailout, which was shrouded within many layers of secrecy. After inking a special economic zone for Bagerville, anxiety and uncertainty were replaced by confidence and a new positive outlook, during which time some within the higher echelons of power ensured that they received a something in return. Not surprising, as some politicians shortly after ended up sending their offspring to some of the most affluent schools internationally.

Further, to sweeten the deal, the government amended the anti-competition laws, regulations and created a special customs zone, allowing for an almost monopoly-like structure to exist and flourish there, with their consent. The voice against these changes were namely the opposition, and Judge Bollxop, who said, "I may have to rescind or alter these decisions in the courts, if I find any ounce of illegal overtures. President Lornae, you may have the voice of the people now, but I will continue to monitor any changes you make to legislations and regulations in finite detail, and look for anything questionable." To this day, we still don't know if maybe an envelope, may have enticed any key decisions.

For a large nation, located in the northern hemisphere in the new world, this was something unthinkable only a few years ago, yet the gods of failed policies and architects of reckless privatizations cheered it. Many voices within the Lornae administration felt that in exchange, "Foreign investment, modernization and infrastructure upgrading will help kick-start all the economic cylinders again." Some within Lornae's cabinet, and even some opposition party members sought - a larger national-status internationally again, within an open-market spectrum, after a few near bankruptcies, currency free fall, falling GDP and heavy reliance on foreign loans and grants from two international banking institutions. After the announcement and signing of the deal, investor and consumer confidence jumped, the foreign reserves increased and the national reputation improved on the world stage.

In the capital, Ophidia, President Lornae continued to hail the strategic alliance, and in one international publication he was quoted as saying, "Through the full utilization of all synergies, and a fully vertical integrated strategic alliance, the government and ViGnChi will create, develop and expand many operations, bringing prosperity to every corner of this nation. Bagerville will also enjoy a nation-like status, sharing within the success, while overall GDP should expand at a robust rate annually for generations to come." Again some within Bagerville began to howl at the pipe dreams, while some echoed sentiments of hope and optimism.

All this began a few years ago, on the fifth floor of the Intra Hotel, in the greater Bagerville-area, which was a card invite event only. Prestigious dignitaries, Bagerville Polytechnic academics and scientists, government, industry officials and a few media moguls were invited under the condition of sworn secrecy on the events inside. The outcome of the talks was vastly cloaked in secrecy, with only half of the details revealed to the public, to allay fears and reduce concerns.

It became a beginning of serenity after the economic chaos, or so many people felt. After all, the full colour prospectus outlined every detail from the extraction, the reserves, the mines, to the finished precision and advanced manufactured products that were meant for the: auto, aerospace, aviation, medical and defence industries.

As if three horsemen had arrived on these shores to conquer the Soma River and the entire higher and lower elevations of the Bagerville-area. An almost picturesque veil of malice began to shroud the area in a grey fog of deceit, under the guise of prosperity. Within the uniquely shaped, Intra Hotel, the new global powerhouse consortium of ViGnChi, was also able to conquer the hearts and minds of many, who feared a descent into an unfathomable economic abyss.

The economic interests and strategic security, were now almost a thing of the past in this nation, where now anything was on the table in the western edges of the prime meridian. As if a new economic world order was imposed, creating a model of servitude, where the workers of Bagerville would in essence become like vassals to an uncrowned authority, were legitimacy was born out of desperation, rather than by a collective will.

The think-tanks, once bonded by more than ideology to political circles, felt the gnawing chokehold of ineptitude, and became silent. Some economists called this deal - Audi, Vide, Tace - or see, hear and be silent, while others whispered, "This is uncompetitive and corrupt." After this signing, the coronation of the new emperor was sealed, and ViGnChi - donned the imperial clothes, and sat at the throne of power in the region, while others became like dependent vassals cloaked in rags.

As the people started moving through the hotel complex, many hands began pushing the automatic buttons, where large double steel doors began to open towards the hallway, boardrooms and through to the banquet space for the event. The nametags of all attendees were all distinctly printed, with the ViGnChi logo and unique symbols adorned around it. Inside the orange colour wall banquet hall, were many tables and seats, with names on them, while at the front was a large monitor screen stage set-up, where government officials, Bagerville Polytechnic and ViGnChi trio were to speak. President John E. Lornae also arrived, though his words were largely drowned out by a few jeers. Just a few weeks before, Lornae took his economic message to the nation, before all the medias stating, "Citizens of this great nation, I come to you this evening with a new message of hope and prosperity. Today we have finalized a very important moment for the nation and Bagerville. ViGnChi International will invest massively for the next 99 years, thus creating opportunities and prosperity, at a time of economic uncertainty and immense change that has grappled the global economy. In Bagerville, ViGnChi has found the right chemistry where economies of scale can flourish, investments can multiply and infrastructure can be built up, as a result of reduced barriers and more free-trade opportunities."

Outside of the room, were a few heavy set characters dressed sharply in suits, security details and even some customers smiling and occasionally answering their various communication devices with long distance rings echoing.

Heading up to the centre of room, towards the front were Thomar Gunthar and Yan Chiu at his side. Boris Vilmajev was a few steps away, and quickly looked towards Jason and gestured politely, "There are some here, who are speculating on the true nature of ViGnChi. I want to assure you that we are firmly committed to all levels of accountability and transparency in all our activities."

Chiu continued, "Since our arrival, ViGnChi has been closely working with all appropriate levels of government in all sectors of our work, with great success and with greater days ahead. Through our multitude of operations, we have developed a wide array of products, to be manufactured here in Bagerville, whose durability, strength, utility and even novelty will spur further growth globally."

At this point, Thomar Gunthar confidently scanned the room, before his aura of arrogance slowly leaned over to Jason and whispered, "No one can reap all the rewards while merely perched on a pedestal whining into a bullhorn. You have to rise above and work hard. Hard work pays off. We have harvested the grape vines and that is why we now sit on a throne and drink from a chalice."

Jason, now holding his hand lens in his right hand, immediately returned a short gesture, with far more tact and promise, "Mr. Gunthar, we have an old saying here too and it boils down to: You reap what you sow. Further, to not respond to that analogy of yours would equate to silence truly being deafening." This comment immediately aroused a few chuckles from many in the room that caught on to the short, back and forth comments.

Gunthar at this point only smiled back at him, before walking to another corner of the room to get himself a drink, and chat with some government officials who were motioning him over.

Nearing the stage now and looking through one of the large windows at the Bagerville landscape, Professor Jason Dallas cussed a few negative comments underneath his coffee stained breath, catching the attention of some government officials and Bagerville Polytechnic staff. Jason noticing that they got his attention then raised his voice a little louder, "This is an absolutely sad hour. It is like a concerted effort to build a new colonial outpost. An economic beachhead for rival superpowers – this is gonna bring nothing but problems."

All around him gave him a questioning quick look before finding their spots at the front. At that point, Jason began to readjust his leather lanyard again, and snapped his metallic hand lens magnifier open and closed a few times, before placing it back into his left breast pocket of his shirt. He then quietly murmured a famous Franz Kafka quote, so that everyone around could hear, "I am a cage, in search of a bird."

Now at the front of the banquet hall near the large screen set up, a chorus of three voices began, "Welcome, dignitaries and guests," Boris Vilmajev, Thomar Gunthar and Yan Chiu opened, in three distinct accents, as in the background more ambient music was now soothing everyone's curiosity. The three were all dressed sharp in snug conservative suits, Vilmajev in dark blue, and Gunthar and Chiu in grey. All rose, and then were seated. Chiu, tall and lanky with neatly polished black leather shoes, stared through his black-framed speckles. His short dark hair was combed to the right as he deeply focused on the surroundings and the people before him.

For Chiu, he grew up in a small community, south of the Gobi Desert, where the opportunities were scarce and the climate was arid. Both elements played a role in shaping his distinct characteristics, as he was a very shrewd businessman, known for turning barren landscapes into economic oasis, with his pragmatic approaches that valued building a dream and fortune, over building trust and teamwork. To him all people were expendable and replaceable, though he did admire Vilmajev and Gunthar enough to unite with them behind a vision and plan.

Vilmajev immediately stretched his posture, and began projecting power with statement, "All of us here have to seize this moment and build on the foundations of growth, with mutual trust and respect." He used strong commanding directives and body language, with arms in the air and side, and clenched fists, while never fidgeting. The creases in his forehead and grey feather-like stains in his rich dark brown hair were empowered by the magnetic laser focus of his hazel eyes and absent facial expressions.

Highly intricate information began to beam across a large screen, followed by satellite imagery, deposits, reserves, soil samples and more technical graphs on all the resources. Then the economic numbers were bolded and enlarged, gaining many loud applauses, as many eyes and ears were now analyzing the info within the prospectus provided and the now quaint ambient backdrop of, J.S. Bach's, Overture No. 3 in D Major - Air, which began flowing through the speakers within the large room.

ViGnChi was comprised of three powerful industrialists, one a former oligarch making his fortune from the resource industry, the other made his mark in advanced manufacturing with an engineering background, while the third was a very successful and powerful building tycoon. The three forged forces a few years ago to make one of the world's strongest multinationals - ViGnChi International - with overseas manufacturing, refining and exploration in the aviation, aerospace, automotive, medical and defence industries.

With massive global growth, they enlisted the services of another resourceful individual to aid in running some of their operations. The person they enlisted was Mr. Vilmajev's old friend and colleague, Mr. Mikhael Igor Gonsev or MIG, an engineer and former military veteran of many battles, with one visible battle scar on his left cheek, who was often described as being, "The man of steel, with brains and brawn, from one of the breakaway regions of the breadbasket, above the Black Sea."

It was like a multi-pronged strategic attack on the world market, to corner all the biggest spending economic cylinders. With the Q90 compound they could become powerful economically, employ thousands around the globe and develop new technologies to replace those from the past century. Yet there were some in suspicion, that small threads or elements, were also going to fuel secret military machines, or sell strategically sensitive advanced manufactured components internationally to the highest bidder, to cause nations to further increase defence spending, thus increasing their share of the global market.

For nearly two hours, various speakers were brought up to the front to present supportive information on various views and concerns, from both the government, academic and business spectrums. Bagerville's Mayor Joe Bohlm made his ceremonial journey, more for the photo-op, than for being present. To him, it was now more important to always meet with the higher powers, rather than serving the people he was elected to do.

Joe spoke for less than two minutes, "Thank you, ViGnChi for your tremendous investments and opportunities in our nation. Thank you, President Lornae for bringing this deal to fruition." Missing within his short speech was a simple mention, or even gratitude to the people of Bagerville, for being the new home of this economic entity. Jason Dallas than took the microphone and requested, "I ask our elected officials and ViGnChi to show Bagerville more respect. We need more transparency and accountability." He further dug his heels in, when he proclaimed, "Many of us would also like to see more corporate social responsibility and environmental protection mechanisms put in place, by everyone." During this ruckus, Gonsev gave Jason a few silent and questioning looks, before shaking his head and focusing back to the presentation. Bagerville Polytechnic President Richard Sula was also not too impressed by Jason, though respected his decision to voice his concerns in an educated manner.

Slowly the double doors be began to close, and only those inside, to this day, know the entire contents that were revealed in the last hour. Many speculations pointed to Jason, having a few heated and tense moments with both Vilmajev and Gunthar. At one point, one of the attendees heard Vilmajev say, "Professor Dallas, you would be far more likeable, if you only focused your energies on more positive things, like joining us make Bagerville great, rather than continually attack us."

Jason quickly became unhinged at that comment, and lashed back, "Our way of life was just fine before you guys arrived. We didn't need you. You needed our resources and our land."

At that point, Gunthar jumped in and denigrated Jason, "Before we came you were just a backwards waste bin. Now you are a jewel in the eyes of the world."

Then Jason retaliated back at Gunthar with, "We were all quite happy with the way of life we had. We were communal, content and family-centric, and not corrupted by false idols. To us the harvest of corn, wheat and grapes on our ancestral lands, was far more valuable than those materials in the Q90." The rest of their discussion was not heard, as near the end, the doors were closed firmly shut.

CHAPTER 3
THE SUNDIAL

"How fast do you think we can go," Matt began rhythmically mimicking a repetitive up-tempo chorus, jacked up to six on the radio dial, by his buddy Tim. Tim Zelk came from an agricultural family in Bagerville, who had many acres of land once, growing corn and wheat. That all changed for the Zelk family, just a few years ago, as most of their land was expropriated for the sake of some new developments, and a rail spur heading towards the new airport. After being quietly paid very little for their lands, most of the Zelk family members reluctantly found new employment opportunities, at some of the ViGnChi contractors, while others within the information technology industry in Bagerville. Now with music flowing through his veins, Matt was erratically twisting and veering in all directions on the steering, causing the tires to spin on the asphalt, gravel, dirt and grass - like a sandblasting tool. At this point his baseball cap fell off his head, which he quickly snatched and tossed behind them onto one of the empty backseats.

Housed within the four wheel, hard top jeep, the two of them began a detoured sail home across many of Bagerville's rural roads, near the Soma, after their afternoon classes ended. Past the steep bends and curves, a few leafy napkins and blue rubber bands found a new home on the roadway, after flying effortlessly through an open window in the jeep. All was forgotten and no one paid attention, asides from an elderly pedestrian shaking his head, and a couple of teenagers walking by, who calmly picked up the litter and disposed of it in a waste bin.

"Take it down a notch Matt, this week is just beginning," barked Tim, who was now getting a tad annoyed. With the wind, dust and descending sun still baking his right arm in the front seat, he began to worry about Matt's erratic maneuvering as they started bouncing and swaying with the four large rubber wheels moving like hungry saw blades in everything they contacted. Now scraping and bouncing on the concrete curbs, the jeep blazing around some contours narrowly missing a couple kids on their longboards on the sidewalk.

Tim got a little irate at this point, after seeing the two kids dive to the side, hitting the grass to avoid a possible collision, yelling at Matt sternly, "Dude, slow down! You're burning through the roads like a demon for the last ten minutes. You're start to remind me of my dad, when he used to thresh our old wheat fields with the combine a few years ago."

Easing off the accelerator and focusing more, Matt apologized, smiled and said, "We're almost there," as he slowly nudged the gearshift down to the first gear, now paying attention to a plaza, a safe lane change and the approaching entrance.

Tim quizzed him with a laugh now, "Where's almost there?" Without words, but a sheer point in the vertical direction, Matt marked it out clearly to Tim, with first his index finger, than with a smile he gave him the middle, before an uproar of laughter ensued.

The message was clear. Tim, now fully realizing a drink before home was gonna happen now, slowly shook his head in disbelief, before questioning himself, "How do I always get myself into this? Now we're gonna soak a few down and feel the pinch of paper missing from the wallet." The jeep with two occupants, slowly approached the desired destination, before turning into a parking slot, where they were going to meet up with a friend over beers at The Sundial. Across the street were some new and old developments, a reminder of the past and future in both architecture and economic progress. An older, now abandoned building had a chain linked fence wrapped around it, where people liked to lock their bikes around. It rattled, and old brush grew through it, and around the rusty old posts resting within the neatly landscaped and manicured grass, with decorative lights along a pedestrian sidewalk. Beside it stood, a six-storey modern and chic building, which had mixed commercial suites and retailers.

"Well, I guess a beer, before we get home, will be alright," Tim looked up towards the passenger side visor, exhaling partially, before putting his right hand at the door to step out and walk into the bar. The Sundial was a well-known, small social hangout for locals. It was a great place to drink beers, grab a bite, play pool and listen to the jukebox, or just chill in the atmosphere. Weekends were always packed with the town's crowd, in for a round or two, and a great place to meet and share some Bagerville memories. The old welcome rubber matt at the entrance counted numerous feet cross its path, before the doors swung open. Heck, it was in the same plaza as Bagerville Foods, the Credit Union and directly across the street from one of the towns few reasonable, and still honest licensed mechanics and auto sales lots. Parked across the street was always the nicest looking cherry red tow truck, from an era long gone, as if a trophy left out in the open. Throughout the town, there was also lots of fresh asphalt, newly designed curbs and sidewalks, along with newly planted trees that dotted the surroundings. Some old light posts still remained, giving the town not only an aesthetic dimension, but also an ambient backdrop to the town's library, built decades ago, where serenity and the thirst for knowledge of intriguing minds could meet.

Across their travel path, less than a kilometre away, Tim noticed the pylons that were spread out near the tripods, trucks and other yellow heavy-duty construction equipment, by the nearly completed extension of the railway link. Tim felt an emotional tug at the scene, "Matt, that was once my family's land, where that link is running through. That was once ours. Remember the corn and wheat fields? Now it's a field of rails." That railway link was going to connect all the way up from the upper elevations of the Q90, to the southern edges, passing through all the industrial quarters, rail yards and then towards the Bagerville Airport-area. It was Gunthar and Vilmajev's idea to, "Better integrate all the raw material area mining areas, with the smelters, factories, manufacturing facilities and warehouses with a rail line, that would connect better to Bagerville Airport, the Rail Yards and the ports in all direction." Quite a few townsfolk had their land expropriated for these new developments, and many were not happy, but took the money and grudged quietly to only a few that would listen. The Voss family had many acres expropriated as well for roads; Bohlm just issued the documents and a cheque that was a fraction of the value. At a recent town hall meeting, Rob Voss got up and shouted, "Bohlm, we once trusted you. How do you sleep at night, knowing you wrecked the lives of many in your hometown? This cheque is a fraction of what my family's land is worth and you know it. But I'll cash it in, and give the funds to my son, Vlad for his education, so hopefully one day he won't have to go through the pain you put me through. You'll be seeing a lot more of my face at the protests." Many of the other townsfolk also voiced their concerns - the Moltracheen's, the Zelk's, as well as Jason Dallas, yet Bohlm just listened and didn't say a word. New developments and infrastructure projects kept sprouting up all within a stones throw away from each other, in this Mecca, now also bound together by new and expanding airport and cargo warehouses.

Roars from a twin engine jet coming in from overseas, could be heard over the well lit and beckoning, The Sundial sign, as it began its smoother than usual descent, towards the Bagerville airport. At the same time, The Sundial's double doors swung open as well with Matt and Tim making their way in, and finding their path to their usual Lions Lair area. Both were now laughing, while digging their hands deeper in their pockets searching for more polymer bills, rather than the keys, loose change or bank cards in their wallets.

Vladimir Voss, or Vlad was just slipping his mobile phone back in his vest, already on his second beer and smiling at the two of them, before quizzing them with, "I was checking the arrivals at the airport on my phone. What took you so long?" Extending his hand for a brotherly handshake, Matt opened up with, "Dude, I was so busy the other day, working on an espresso and a project at the Meze Cafe. Sorry, I wasn't social."

"No worry, I was in a bit of a hurry too," Vlad quickly shot back.

At that point, Matt, Tim and Vlad began exchanging a few words, before Matt grabbed a beer off the table, took a sip and proclaimed, "Like good old days, ah boys? Once we were the aspiring information technology gurus."

"Interests change, and writing was my calling. My dad always tells me - do what drives you, and then put everything into it," Vlad reminded his friends. The conversation then continued within their corner, albeit at a quieter tone about various topics ranging from: ViGnChi, The Observer and some interesting files. Within ten minutes, the conversation changed again, as a large cold pitcher of beer, with three mugs landed on the table before their eyes and parched pallets. Before the first mug was filled, Matt got up and walked over to the bar, to clear a tab and order some food for the boys.

The Sundials owner, Frank Moltracheen was a Bagerville native too, like both his parents. Everyone knew everyone in that town, and very well. "How's the parents Matt," asked the still athletic, full of hair and life Bagerville native, as he glanced over from behind the counter, taking the cash and tossing the change on the counter back, while cleaning up the work area with a small rag. "They're doing alright, you should pop by the house sometime for a coffee," Matt responded, before heading back to his seat. Beer mugs clanged to that comment, and the three took their honorary and hearty swigs of beer, before letting out a few roars and belches. Frank rubbing a cloth against the counter still, while cracking a smile and looking up towards the windows responded, "I think I'll give your dad a call soon. We go back. Actually there are a few of us here in Bagerville that go back. We were once like brothers, doing everything growing up. Back in the days, Beth and me had Moltracheen Estates and the best vineyards in this whole area. It's been a little rough since she passed. Ah, memories. Jim Dallas, your great-grandfather. He was a hell of a man. A father figure. A teacher and a friend."

A warm feeling overcame Matt upon hearing those words, but he quickly relaxed into the present atmosphere and simply responded, "Frank, your awesome. Never change."

A couple of regulars in flannel and t-shirts, were holding a few darts by the barrel and points in one hand, and half-litre bottles of beers in the other, about six feet away from the circular bristle bulls eye numbered board, while the jukebox was oozing with sweet and soothing laid back melodies. The reddish and dark brick walls were covered with memories of photos and autographed pictures, while the billiards tables were busy, as the cues clicked, knocked and pelted eight ball numbered games before a quick cue rub, and continuing with other racked games.

A big screen TV was having its channels turned from the bar a few times, from a Baseball game to some breaking news story again - something about the ViGnChi split, Gunthar's new venture and some possible breach of information investigation. Everyone was partially viewing and absorbing the big news event, though not fully paying attention, while some were tuning into only a few keywords being mentioned. The Sundial was loaded with patrons all the time now, as the economic expansion helped fuel new economic migrants to the booming Bagerville area.

The staff expanded to six now, including Frank, and the way he mussed it up was, "I get alot of hardworking people that work in the Q90 for ViGnChi passing through these doors lately, almost all day. They drink. They eat. They pay. They leave. Business is good. I like to keep it that way. No hassles. No problems. It's different than making wine for a living, but that's another story." During Frank's diatribe, one of the kitchen staff waltzed quietly over to the Lion's Lair with a loaded tray of tacos, wings, wedges and veggies, where three sets of hungry eyes were enlarged, and waiting to dig in.

The topic of conversation continued amongst the boys and Frank, as to the unbelievable growth the area has seen, due in large part of the huge investments, and many times at the detriment and expense of some great people in his town. Shortly after, Frank began to delve into an old great fire in Bagerville nearly two decades ago. An old school literally caught fire, exposing some to toxic fumes and quite possibly asbestos, which was not removed from some areas of the upper floors. Thankfully there were no casualties, though there was a lot of damage and media attention for Bagerville.

Continuing, "Matt, your father was near the area doing some research project then, many moons ago, when he noticed things going up. He saved a person. Got his leg done in bad. That was like the most disgusting dark plume of smoke I ever recalled billowing. We could all see it, as far back the Moltracheen Estates stretched back then. I'll never forget the nasty scent that lasted for hours, and made many people sick. Your dad made it to the news."

All nodded, before many hands and fingers began attacking the bowl of tacos, dipping then within the salsa dish, before consuming with excitement. Matt still thinking about Frank's last comment, just tightened his eyes and facial muscles and simply replied, "I know. He saved my mother from the flames. She was just beginning to teach. That was the first time they met. Now she uses an inhaler, as she's developed respiratory problems." The table now went silent, as all reflected on those words for a few moments.

Snapping back, with a little more of an upbeat swing, Matt emphatically assured everyone with, "They're both solid. Amazing parents and friends I can talk to." Now leaning back in his seat, and with his right hand rubbing the small growth on his chin, he continued, "My dad's more quieter at times. Sometimes, I catch him fading into past moments, before snapping out. Bohlm cancelling the annual Bagerville Harvest Fair was also sacrosanct to my dad. Then again, being a professor and dealing with so many people lately at the Polytechnic, politicians and ViGnChi. He's the town's torchbearer for the protests and demonstrations, and I think there is a lot of merit to that. But then again, sometimes I think he'd rather just teach or do research, than deal with all the nonsense." All were just jabbing into small talk again about various issues around Q90, before Matt sighed and continued, "Dad and me think. Forget it. Maybe another time." Once again, beer mugs clanged and the three took another few swigs and chuckled at the area near the centre of the bar.

Below the wide circular luminous light in the centre of the bar was a green and black pool table. A couple of slender built workers were slowly calculating their next moves with their beers in hand. Click, clack and smacking could be heard repetitively along with a few brief emotionally charged comments.

For about four seconds, an undisturbed silence followed, so that one could possibly only hear a pin drop, before Vladimir declared, "I'm going to delve into this a little further in the next Bagerville Observer," as his eyes became fixated at the low hanging wrought iron six candle lights in the middle of The Sundial.

The Bagerville Observer was the community long running weekly, established almost a century ago, by the town's founder William Bagerville. Vlad, who was studying journalism at Bagerville Polytechnic, was a contributing writer who periodically did columns and interviews on events affecting the community. This was going to be an investigative challenge for him, as he was planning a career in journalism after graduation. Vlad was a very bright and intuitive student, initially studying information technology with Matt and Tim, before finding his true calling in writing in his first year at Bagerville Polytechnic.

Matt was formulating a thought stream, after hearing Vlad mention an article he was working on, and finally snapped with a comment, "My father always says – things were better before in Bagerville. Before the massive economic transformation. I believe him."

Feeling the effects of a couple mugs of beer, Matt now drifted into a childhood memory with a jerk of emotion. He remembered sitting by a wooden pier, fishing on the meandering edges of the Soma River for hours with his parents, reminiscing about the town, near those once quiet waters and clear skies. They now clanged their mugs again, while noticing a now empty pitcher before them.

At this point, Matt slowly sensed many shady characters amongst them listening, so he nudged Vlad and Tim, and slightly whispered something of grand importance again, regarding some documents, individual and business dealings at Q90, that no one asides those at the table heard.

Another exhale and Matt ended by shaking his head, closing his eyes and muttering a little louder now, "Bagerville was like a beautiful meadow, a quiet paradise. It was more laid back, more family centric and communal. I agree with my dad, it is growing into a monster of sorts. We have to bring it back. The protests can only do so much, but we are being drowned out." At that point, Matt threw the jeep's keys on the table, and asked for a coin toss, as to who was more sober to spin the wheels back home, as it was definitely a wrap for the night.

Movements could be heard from the back of the bar - the last table to be precise. A few chairs shuffled and a big fellow in a black leather jacket with a gruff accent got up to use the bathroom located down the hall. His other two pals were chatting amongst themselves, drinking beer and playing cards at the table.

Another tall and lanky male, with long hair, pushed his chair slightly from another table at the back, almost losing his balance. As he regained his composure, he let out a thunderous belch, which was heard by all, and headed for the jukebox machine, while struggling to fish some coins from his pockets.

At the other end of the bar, a gruff and half tanked male voice, who was a nephew of Frank's, near another billiards called out, "Two more pints over here Frank." He then winked and whispered over to his uncle, "I can't call you Uncle Frank here?" Mark and his girlfriend Sally were shooting a game and wanted at least another beer, before they'd start heading back home. Sally was starting to bat her eyelashes slower, while Mark's entire left hand was coated with blue chalk powder from the two pool cubes he was holding. "Mark, I'm afraid you had a little too much today. I'm cutting you off. I reckon you got work early tomorrow. Something to drive, I'm sure. I spoke with your father earlier and he mentioned you have a new driving job. As a matter of fact, I'm calling you a cab now, and you can leave your vehicle here in the parking lot. It'll be all right sitting here until tomorrow, " Frank firmly outlined the deal, while beginning to dial for a cab.

At this point, from the Lions Lair table area, two eyes and ears honed in on the conversation with a slight smile. Without noticing too much in the bar, Mark paused and stared out the window, where a heavy set lady was standing by the grocery store, resting a few grocery bags on sidewalk, while she lit a cigarette. For a moment it reminded him of his late Aunt Betty, his Uncle Frank's late wife, who passed away a few years ago, after The Moltracheen Estates were sold-off and the land on it expropriated. Mark scratched his forehead, shifted his eyes back to his surroundings and finally submitted to the exit game, by declaring, "It's time to call it the night. I'm starting to see things. Maybe I have had too much to drink."

With his eyes a tad blurry while looking around the bar now, Mark continued, "You're right Uncle Frank. I got a load to haul tomorrow, and early." His tired feet then began tapping at the baseboards and floors, while he still mustered some energy to pull off a half smile, as he held off on a run to men's room. Looking at Frank one last time, he confessed, "Its time to recharge the batteries. I'm leaving. I'll be by sometime tomorrow to pickup my wheels."

At that time, a few older regular patrons came through, including a cab driver from the town, popping in to pickup a few patrons. "Frank, you won't have to worry about me taking a cab home tonight," a chuckling driver proudly announced as he walked in and waited for his two customers. Scanning the bar, the driver continued, "Frank, It looks like a big night again." Frank nodded back and smiled, before acknowledging, "Good business. All the customer's have money and they like to spend it. Yes sir. All these patrons you see in the bar like to drink. If I still had my winery today, I'd be out of stock. At times, I've also been offered more than the tip of the hat to ignore some of the theatrics, I see. Ah, that's another story." At that point both Mark and his auburn haired beauty Sally, stumbled very cautiously out of The Sundial and into the waiting cab outside, and took their journey home.

CHAPTER 4
A PARTING OF WAYS

After a few years at the helm of ViGnChi's engineering, and after the parting of Thomar Gunthar, Mikhael Igor Gonsev was approached and courted by one familiar face - and a host of headhunting firms with offers. He simply declined, until the caveats of high rank and authority were thrown on a gold platter for him. The elements of discipline and power really had his antennas tuned in, as it reinforced some important traits learned in his military years, and during the civil unrest in his former homeland.

The other traits that interested him, was the offer to share in the building of an organization geared towards advanced manufacturing in - aerospace and defence. He had exchanged numerous emails back and forth with Gunthar, regarding some ideal propositions. He wanted to ensure that any final, and firm commitment was solidified with a concrete path moving forward.

After having lost his wife Svetlana and daughter Olga, during the insurgency in his former homeland, his career was the only thing that made him tick and kept him sane now. It was over a decade ago, when a civil war erupted and chaos unfolded, where he had to abandon his family, home and career to fight for what in his heart and mind was the right thing to do - fight for freedom. Many like-minded foreigners arrived to their cause, some from the Mediterranean and Balkan nations. His battalion consisted of many volunteers from all points of the globe, including Yuri and Nick - who once also had stints as legionnaire fighters in the Maghreb - yet both never made it home alive, after the last battle.

Gonsev's hometown, near the Black Sea bore some of the heaviest fighting, and some aerial bombardments took out entire sections of his street, including his house. On a very cold April morning, his wife Svetlana, and daughter Olga who was just seven at the time, were hiding within the cellar for safety. The extent of the damage and the collateral damage was so horrific that it forever scared him, deeper than the gash he received on his left cheek from a hand-to-hand fight with a soldier on the frontlines.

The rains of April always fall as if tears from the heavens, and when he sees them, it forever reminds him of the worst funeral he ever had to attend. To this day, he still carries a photo of Svetlana and Olga in his wallet, while within his home is a large family portrait sitting in his living room, everyday reminding him of the life he once had. It was over a decade ago, yet the memories still remain strong, and the only thing that drives him now is his career in a new continent.

Within the past week, he had continued some further secret consultations with Gunthar and the charting out of a future map, after dropping off some documents for him at his place. Focusing on two core industries to him was the way to go, though the first thing, and the right thing, was to tender his resignation first. He sent a quick email to Vilmajev requesting a short and informal meeting regarding some professional developments.

Vilmajev and Gonsev had known each other for many years, before he came to ViGnChi to head the engineering divisions. Prior to the scheduled meeting Vilmajev already had a great suspicion that MIG would depart, as some rumours already began to circulate that Gunthar was seeking a partner. Vilmajev was mostly pragmatic with a laser business focus, which clicked with his other partner Chiu. The two were used to continuous changes, and already had a joint discussion on revamping some key operations, in light of the structural changes that were beginning.

As Gonsev left his residence in a nice quiet suburb of Bagerville, he slowly drove his car admiring the surroundings with a clear view of the entire terrain, from the lower edges to the higher elevations and grandness of the Soma, which twisted and swirled around the area. Some of the foliage of the vast trees, that lined some stretches, were changing from their lush green to a mixed reddish, brown and yellow, while the spruce and pines still retained their blue to evergreen aesthetic.

Driving further towards his destination, he marvelled at some of the town's last remaining farm fields, where plough-tilled chunks of dark soil, mixed with clay laid turned over beside the countless bales of hay. Those dark, gold and green images also reminded him of his old homeland, once considered a breadbasket. Scanning further in the now partly cloudy distance, he noticed developments, new and old, and then the majestic mountains that peaked high in the Q90 horizon.

As he drew even closer to the offices, he could see the approaching twelve floor tall business complex, mostly made of glass and steel, which was the ViGnChi central nervous system, close to the mines, factories and the warehouses. You couldn't miss the unique logo, that was soon to change, and the big letters - ViGnChi. It stood out as the tallest structure in the landscape with antennas, dishes and repeaters attached to the rooftop.

Within a few minutes, he pulled into the executive parking, and placed his car in the first row, a couple of spots from the doors leading to the entrance. As he got out of the car, with some documents in hand, he began to slowly pace his steps and thoughts, before entering through the doors. A hack at their R&D department still bothered him, yet he knew eventually it would be resolved. As he entered through the doors, he checked in with the security desk personnel, who greeted him, and then headed towards the elevator, where he pushed the button for the 8th floor.

Slow and melodic music hummed in the background from the speakers, as he was making his way in the elevator and eight floors up, until the doors opened. As the elevator doors opened, he noticed that he was only a few steps from another desk, with staff. At the desk were a few men and women congregating with documents in hand, under the backdrop of a decorative new ViChi logo and large decorative clock with Roman numerals.

On the 8th floor, those that recognized him, seated behind the front desk on the phones and computers, once again greeted him with smiles and small pleasantries. Gonsev continued walking towards the boardroom, past the carpeted hallway and walls covered with - important portraits of awards, projects and major news stories from global media. One of the young ladies from the front desk stepped out to walk with him, "Good day Mr. Gonsev, it's nice to see you here. I just got back from a recent vacation down south, it was great - the sun, food and beach. I'm going to take a bit of walk with you, as Mr. Vilmajev is on a call right now with a client. I'll knock and advise him, before you go in." The young lady continued to walk with Gonsev towards the boardroom, before she arrived in front of the double-doors and knocked a few times. Vilmajev was finishing up with a call, as she peered in and announced, "Mr. Gonsev has arrived for your meeting, sir." Vilmajev, just smiled and asked, "Please send him in. Thank You." Gonsev, at this point politely smiled and thanked the young lady, before wishing her, "Have a wonderful day. Take more vacations. Life is short. Enjoy every minute."

Within another minute, Gonsev entered the boardroom, where Vilmajev was waiting for him, with a couple of cognacs and a questioning smile.

Dressed sharply in a blue conservative suit and red tie with his scar very noticeable, he opened with, "Thank you, but I won't be having any drinks today. Before I begin, I want to thank you for meeting with me on such short notice on my initiative to discuss some very changes that are unfolding. This is going to be a little difficult, yet necessary."

Vilmajev attentively listened, taking a sip of cognac, while eying some cigars and grabbing the box to offer one to Gonsev, who just nodded his index figure and head, indicating that it was not on the game plan either.

At this point Gonsev continued, "Boris we have known each other for many decades, and I have immense respect for everything you have done for me, yet I have come here today after serious consideration to tender my resignation. I feel it is time that I pursue higher interests with a higher-level authority."

Vilmajev was silent, yet he kept firmly looking at Gonsev, while raising one eyebrow before sitting down, and motioning his hand towards a drink and seat at the table.

Gonsev just shook his head and continued, "That said, I have enjoyed my time here and will always look back with great memories and great accomplishments that we have achieved as a whole. Also, you will always be like a brother to me. You've been there for me on many fronts." At this point, deep down he wanted to have a stiff drink, but he also wanted to have everything remain positive and without the influence of alcohol, which could alter the conversation into a negative light.

He deeply respected Vilmajev, but he felt the right course would be to do it firmly and professionally, while also allowing for the building of future bridges, rather than building walls of mistrust.

Immediately feeling a sense of betrayal, Vilmajev took another gulp of his cognac and poured an immediate second before confessing, "MIG, I hope a pathetic R&D data breach isn't bugging you that much? I have nothing to worry about. They'll find the hacker soon enough. I brought you here because - I trusted your knowledge, and your uncompromising moral compass that guides you. I would have given you the world, though I know your heart is elsewhere now. I know you too well. I will respect your decision, though I only ask that you remain until we reorganize. I already had the feeling you were going to leave as well, once Gunthar made his decision. You see MIG, Gunthar came here with us more as a third party to financially allow us to absorb such a large project. It was an agreement in principle, that once things were established, he would venture on his own. We all sat down with Mayor Bohlm and President Lornae, along with a few of his cabinet ministers recently in Bagerville, so they're in the know of the changes. As for Gunthar, his ultimate vision is about conquest at any cost. He doesn't care about any rendering. It's all about his ego, and nothing more. There is no emotion in that man. His moral compass is a mirror of himself. So should you go venture with him, remember these words. It's all a game to him, and a game where he must win at any cost. The game is his Achilles Heel - without the game he falls. Be careful what you wish for, because your wish may come true one day."

A few months ago, on a late summer evening, President Lornae flew into Bagerville, from Ophidia, unannounced and with a minimal security detail. He came with a few cabinet ministers and met with Vilmajev,

Chiu and Gunthar, over dinner at the quiet Spirit Bistro, which was closed off to regular patrons and passerbys. A small security perimeter was set-up with dark cars and men in suits scanned the area, causing some rubbernecking in traffic and slowing down many buses in town.

Professor Dallas was just coming back from a lecture at Bagerville Polytechnic and got caught up in a post-rush hour traffic jam, when he got closer to town, he noticed the many dark vehicles, luxurious sedans belonging to the ViGnChi trio, and Bohlm's truck. Jason Dallas flipped his radio dial to see if any news reports came up, but realized that this was an impromptu Lornae meeting at The Spirit Bistro, which neither he, nor Sula were aware of, so he muttered to himself, "Odd that Lornae is in town. Wonder what that's all about. Then again Bohlm's truck is there too. It has to be something."

As he approached closer to The Spirit Bistro, he noticed the silhouettes of all of them sitting behind a large table with drinks, as they were examining some documents, before he heard the sound of steel grinding from a distance that quickly distracted him to focus on the road again. A few rail cars were shunting some cargo on a spur in the distance of the Q90, where he noticed thick white and grey plumes of pollution making their ascent to the highest clouds on the humid and moonlit night.

Back inside The Spirit Bistro, Lornae and his loyal cabinet ministers were informed of the split before hand, and the two entities that were to be formed. Lornae listened attentively, and then stood up to take off his blazer and placed it over his chair, before sitting down again to engage in further dialogue with all parties present. Bohlm was mostly quiet the entire time, just listening.

Outside the front doors, the patio was set up, yet all chairs and tables were empty, as two security staff were standing uncomfortably in suits, making sure that no unexpected guests would enter, to the closed door meeting inside. Lornae looked at Vilmajev first and firmly said, "No dinner. Let's just cut to the chase. Hammer it home. What are we looking at? What is the new game plan?" Vilmajev and Gunthar both smiled and said simultaneously, "A new game. Two for the price of one?" The meeting went on into the late hours of the morning, before it was concluded and an agreement was met. Lornae gave his word, that everything would remain the same. Bohlm just kept smiling the whole time, before he uttered his famous words, "What's in it for me?"

Gonsev listened attentively to Vilmajev who narrated the events from a few months ago, and reminded him, " I am the master of my own destiny, and I'm capable of holding my own weight in any given situation." After hearing those words, Vilmajev rose from his seat and extended his arms wide before interjecting, "MIG, this structure is complex. It's intertwined. It's like a web of entities all conjoined in the Q90. We will still be bound and we can still work together in many capacities. Take for instance the auto industry. We can still work on some advanced manufacturing projects, rather than outsource to third party unreliable and inefficient regions. Chiu, and me were recently at an automotive trade show in the Middle East, and have inked some manufacture to specification projects. These projects are high-end and upscale components for some auto giants for their luxury edition models, totalling perhaps 100,000 units. That is just one contract we inked, there are many others in the works."

Both then smiled at one another with sceptical eyes, and refrained from digging into any wounds, but rather focused on the other individual about to join them from down the hallway. Just before Chiu would enter the room, Gonsev decided to walk over to the edges of the table, near a window and glance out at the Bagerville horizon and smile, before taking a glass and pouring some spring water into to it. He then turned to Vilmajev, and raised his glass and said to him, "Let's toast, even if I'm just drinking water today." A few smiles ensued, before both toasted to health and prosperity for both.

As the centre of power cleaved further down the middle, the discussions behind closed doors continued once Chiu entered the room a few minutes in. They spoke at lengths about numerous hurdles, before Vilmajev interjected again, "We need to work together in some capacities in the future, in order to take advantage of major opportunities, which will benefit both organizations." All three agreed, then Gonsev proposed, "We should continue to share the information technology services department, and unite our synergies, particularly in the new robotics division."

Standing beside Vilmajev and Chiu, Gonsev continued speaking, "My desires are to work on more challenging projects, which require great detail. These new advanced manufacturing projects, will impact our world in a positive way. The new advanced manufacturing facility will be outfitted with many robotic technologies, increasing the productivity and reducing the costs on many fronts." Chiu listened and observed everything carefully, wanting only to make sure that any transition would be smooth. Chiu then reminded everyone, "I value business details and numbers far more than loyalty and emotions. I love to build and create, rather than give away something or try to heal a wound. I just pitched Mayor Bohlm on a ViChi development within central Bagerville. It's more of a real estate investment, mixed residential and commercial use. I want the land in an area adjacent to the old library in town. He reassured me the permits wouldn't be a problem." Gonsev's presence before Chiu, meant very little, as he knew that there was always another to take his place, while Vilmajev looked at his leaving a little more personal.

All three within the room showcased professionalism and decorum, while exchanging many ideas, though Gonsev could still see that Vilmajev was not entirely happy with his decision to leave. Gonsev and Vilmajev's bonds were almost fraternal, as each of them knew each other's strengths and pains since their formative years. Vilmajev was also at his wedding, his daughter's birth and even at the mournful funerals. After university, when Vilmajev started working on some large automotive and industrial projects, he offered Gonsev contracts in a town west of Urals, where he let him oversee the a few key departments. This parting of ways was a difficult moment, though their friendship would continue and ending things diplomatically rather than having bridges burned made for a smoother path going forward, no matter which way the roads take them.

CHAPTER 5
THE DATA BREACH

Days before and less than three miles away at a secure and unsuspecting coffee house, a laptop computer was on the verge of going online, with a masked dynamic IP address constantly changing to avoid detection. A few hardware components were added to the soup mix, along with encrypted software designed for sneaking in through the back door to acquire important ViGnChi files, right under their noses.

The aromatic nexus of coffees and teas, with hints of lively spirits and pastries, filled The Meze Cafe, creating a welcoming ambience, far away from the noise of a town morphing into a regional economic beast. Low hanging lights, rustic shelves, mahogany tables and Bohemian-like crafts and artwork, gave the abode an appeal to the many seeking refuge and solace, for a soul reviving drink or two. With a deep sigh, a silver cased laptop opened on a brown oval table in this caffeine paradise, where small clusters of artsy people socializing, and the Baristas didn't suspect a thing.

At this time, Vlad was passing by the street doing some quick shopping, and in a hurry noticed Matt through the window at The Meze Cafe, before he flipped him a quick salute and a signal that he'd ring him later on the cell.

After a slight pause for thought, and a laser sharp focus centred on a task to seek and find a treasure trove of documents, two hands rested over a keyboard before his fingers began tapping lengthy sequences. After a few minutes, he paused for a sip of his chamomile tea, which was hot and steaming in his green mug almost becoming welded to the table, beside a neatly folded newspaper to his right. Another sip and his eyes honed on the screen again, before his fingers continued parsing intricate instructions and commands. The son of a non-violent and vocal resistance leader in town, who had a desire to uncover a web of intrigue under a cloak of secrecy, to what he labelled, "A vault of information, that could shake any organization down to its foundations."

Since he was six-years old, he tinkered with programming in his parent's basement. He wasn't interest in rocks and terrains like his father Jason Dallas, or teaching like his mother Gordana, he was fascinated with algorithms, intricate codes and formulas. He also loved music notations, song structures and everything that had a beginning point and end to it. He liked video gaming, and even hacking into small unsuspecting computers, and those interests from a very young age turned to a passion, as he grew older. In Grade 7, he even wrote short scripts and programs for school projects, and helped a local store set-up a database.

Earlier in the week, Matt realized he left a bit of a paper trail in the basement on a table, containing a flowchart and some documents regarding the ViGnChi R&D centre, which Jason stumbled upon with a curious look, and some degree of suspicion, that he may be up to something. Matt remembered his father asking him, "That flowchart and some of those names on those pages downstairs seem to be ascending to a very interesting hierarchy. Is it part of a project of some kind Matt?" Matt quickly downplayed the paper trail with a unconvincing smirk, before emphatically outlining his desires, "Dad, there are a few things I'm exploring, without crossing any redlines. Some things have affected this town, the people I cherish the most, and this nation. I want to help the Zelk, Voss and the Moltracheen's, in anyway I can. I share your deep pain, and I'm just researching some things at this point, as it seems cheap money has corrupted the souls of many around us." Jason just stood back, smiled and told his son, "You'll always know deep in your heart on what is right, what is just, and what is wrong. Yesterday, I ran into one of your instructors, Professor Tahlson on the second floor, he mentioned that you're one of his brightest students. I told Tahlson, that you said, "I want to be above the pack. I want to be an innovator and a leader within my field, rather than just another employee in a company doing a job for years without any reward." Without going into too much detail, Tahlson then mentioned, that you expressed a real entrepreneurial spirit, "Mr. Tahlson, one day I would love to acquire, maintain and even lease or buy a large server, and offer information technology services to small and mid-size enterprises in Bagerville after graduation." Jason looked at his son with enthusiasm and stated, "Matt, I'm behind you all the way." With a sense of pride, Matt looked his dad in the eyes and extended his hand to give him a high five, before going to give him a big hug, "Thanks, Dad. I love you."

Those thoughts and words were from earlier in the week, but now for greater part of almost 10 minutes his fingers continued to meticulously send codes and scripts in sequences to a server elsewhere. Matt's heart, mind and fingers worked in unison, under an unsuspecting cloak, in an attempt to retrieve files from a centre, located within the heart of Q90.

Flipping his baseball cap backwards, over his slightly unwashed hair, the genius in the making frowned at his surroundings, and raised his hands for a jovial, yet silent stretch of the arms, before lowering them back to the table and continuing with his plan. Then the final tap of the key, and it was now complete. With a sense of excitement, he smiled, exhaled and got up from his table quickly, heading over to one of Baristas, and ordered an espresso. He needed a quick jolt now, before the avalanche of documents would begin to flood his laptop, with a total of 600 plus Megabytes of precious data. Some documents and files were dated, some were named: From ViGnChi to ViChi: The Transformation, ViGnChi minutes, ViGnChi meetings, Budgets, RFPs, as well as a host of other interesting documents. Further down he also retrieved correspondence, CAD drawings, renderings, designs and a few documents stemming from Gunthar and Gonsev's email conversations regarding future contracts.

Matt's eyes were in disbelief, and his mouth almost froze, after seeing all these files he was about to acquire. His thoughts shifted to Vlad, and he decided to forward some of those files to his Bagerville Polytechnic email, with a few notes. In one another separate email, he also asked him, "Maybe you can leak some of these interesting items out in The Bagerville Observer?" He then also decided to upload a few pictures from his cell, which he snapped recently from a distance while observing - Gunthar's place. A few contained someone in his backyard, rustling around with what looked like some hardcopy documents in a yellow manila folder. At the time, he was just driving his jeep home from class one afternoon and noticed something very strange near Gunthar's place. He noticed Gonsev rustling around in his backyard with some documents. He quickly parked his jeep in an area not too visible across the street from Gunthar's house, and began taking pictures and video clips. He remembers stating, "This is crazy. This is priceless - Gonsev in Gunthar's backyard. I wonder what that's all about? I'll just film it and check it out later. It may be worth something one day."

Matt ended up deciding that those pictures and videos may contain something, so he sent them to Vlad with a comment, "Vlad, for all it's worth, check out these attachments. A picture and video clip of Gonsev in Gunthar's backyard. It maybe something, or maybe nothing, but the fact is those two are in a new company together."

On the other end of the spectrum, within the R&D department of ViGnChi, one of the heads of I.T. Department, was at this time on break, taking a drag of a cigarette and enjoying small talk in the smoking area, outside of his nearby office with a few colleagues, not suspecting or knowing of the breach taking place. After finishing his break, the tall and introverted programmer, with jet black hair and stained teeth, dressed in a dark polo shirt and designer jeans, sat down in his chair, and stared in disbelief into his monitor with alarm, stating, "What the?"

Beside his desk there were a few tall pine bookshelves and steel file cabinets, loaded with manuals, binders and countless data tapes and CDs, all categorically filed under name and date. An open file folder with a few strands of loose paper were scattered over one cabinet, entitled geological and aerial surveys of Bagerville from the past few years.

Down the hall, a small group of domestic and foreign scientists could be seen walking down a corridor to a lab of sorts attire on and binders in hands, chatting, moving slowly and observing displayed products and information.

A few kilometres away, a mountain of data was floating down the screen of a laptop in a coffee house. Back at the R&D department, the programmer was beginning to tense up and parse through the scenario that was unfolding, while slowly placing his right hand over the receiver of the telephone, with a thought on calling Gonsev. With a short burst of puzzlement, the programmer shook his head and angrily muttered, "No. It can't be. Someone has broken in and is copying and retrieving. Files." He kept gazing at the rapid succession of short alpha and numeric scripts racing down the screen. His now reddish reflection was staring back at him through the dark monitor alit, with a language he was quite fluent with - hacking.

For almost another twenty minutes, the programmer tried to find out what happened, but by then he became consumed by anger, stress and perspiration, which was running like rain water down his back. His now clammy hand grabbed the phone this time, and he dialled ten digits, while with his other fist, he bashed objects into bits off his desk. Those digits turned to tones, before the other end picked up and the programmer revealed, "Mr. Vilmajev, we have a problem! Someone has hacked into our system. A data breach. I'm gonna call Gonsev after I get off the phone with you."

Further details of the conversation couldn't be heard, as the printers in the lab began spitting out garbled pages of data, yet there were suspicions that the Bagerville authorities, the government and some clients of ViChi, were requested to be involved and notified, as some of the information may have been extremely sensitive. Someone had broken into the R&D centre, where countless documents, correspondence and sensitive designs for many projects were kept. Further, countless other sensitive files from the personal computers of Vilmajev, Gunthar, Gonsev, Chiu and others were affected as well.

The programmers fingers continued typing on the keypad at a frantic pace, with all facial muscles, shoulders and neck stiffened. He then paused for a moment to exhale from his now reddened face, before keying a final sequence of algorithms into a program, and then waiting a minute to see if there was a response. His right hand fetched the phone again, and dialled another ten digits, while loosing his calm and blurting, "I have to inform Gonsev. This is ugly."

Gonsev saw the R&D name on his cell, so he quickly answered it from his desk, "Gonsev here. What's up?" He could hear static and garble crackling from his cell phone, before he heard the programmer relay a disturbing message, "Someone hacked into our system. I'm trying to find the point of origin." Within less than a minute of the conversation, terse expressions were overshadowed by bursts of profanities, as both were trying to figure out who would do something like this. Gonsev made a request, "Keep a lid on things, and find any location that the hack may have come from, and if there are any surveillance videos of the point of origin." For a few minutes he sat at his desk, where photos of his deceased wife and daughter stood facing him, he pondered many things while shaking his head. His eyes almost became cold, distant, yet professionalism remained within his conscience, as he tried to search within as to who would want to do this and why? His search was fruitless, as he couldn't think of anyone that would want to do this, yet he now knew the right thing would be to inform all involved, while still wanting answers as to who was behind this. Expressing his desire to get to the bottom of things, he suggested to the programmer, "If need be, use all resources you may need, but find out who the perpetrator is, and get back to me."

The Programmer gave Gonsev a solemn oath, "I promise you, we will find the culprit. Right now I'm getting a slight signal that it may have originated at The Meze Cafe. Whoever this is, hacked over 60 Megabytes worth of documents. I'm going to try to double down on everything and verify. Give me a few hours, I'll get back to you if anything changes."

Once again, Gonsev took in the information and parsed a keyword, "600 Megabytes of information stolen, but why?" He took a few deep breaths before in full agreement with the programmer, he simply requested in an authoritative tone, "Please get back to me, the moment you find out. I'll inform Gunthar myself, as Vilmajev already knows and he's already notified Chiu. This data breach is not going to go over to well with some people. Gunthar is going to go ballistic."

Now the programmer was trying in vain to pin point the source and unmask the intruder, though like a thief in the night, the hacker left without a confirmed trace.

CHAPTER 6
TEACH AND MEET

After presenting slide presentations with key points on the screen, which the students scurried to absorb as the class progressed, Professor Jason Dallas decided to finish the Geophysical Engineering 302 lecture in an unconventional way with a chalk.

Looking towards the students, Jason began, "I noticed all of you diligently taking the notes down, therefore I have decided to finish the lecture with another important element to the mix. Calcium Sulphate. Some would think, the Plaster of Paris and Gypsum together, I like to think of it as the material made from both - chalk. An important tool for any scribe or student." At this point there were a few chuckles in each corner, before Jason continued arduously to expand on the lesson, indicating, "Some materials and compounds when mixed together create one thing, while sometimes they can also be used to create something entirely different."

For almost another thirty minutes into the lecture, Jason continued his archaic method of rapidly scribbling complex data on the chalkboard. A few seconds later, he was interrupted, when a slight crack in the chalk caused a shrill screech and white powder to crumble all over his hand. Looking up into the corner of the classroom, towards the clock, he slowly rubbed a strand of powder over an eyebrow, before crushing the remainder of the chalk against board with his palm, into pieces. He shook his head and then said, "This chalk powder will not be placed under any slides, or viewed under a Petrographic microscope today." A few chuckles were heard from some of the students, realizing that he was trying to now poke fun at the fact he broke the chalk.

His lecture was near ending, when he tried to convey an ending message, "All things have break points, or moments when stress or friction can reduce their effectiveness." The students without peeping just stared at him with a look of disbelief, as he didn't seem to be in one of his chipper moods now.

Sensing a bit of stress, he slowly took a few steps towards his desk and sat down, while the class continued copying the last bits of information and examined their notes. Leaning back in his chair, he took a deep breath, then exhaled and reached for his mug of now cold coffee, which he began to press against his twitching lips. To sooth his discomfort, he began to fidget with his metallic hand lens like a pacifier of sorts. He popped the lens back and forth a few times, before he placed it back into his shirt pocket. He then glanced over at his mobile phone on his desk, "Two messages already? One from Matt and the other from Gordana."

The room was silent, with just eyes on him and not a word coming from the students. Then a student at the back quizzed Jason with a short, yet direct question, "Is everything alright professor?" Jason just looked at all of the class and responded, "Yes, continue with the notes and begin modeling and calculation work on exercise 1 on page 434 for now, as I won't be boring you all with any further geological theories and stories of tectonic plate shifting today." The students continued scribbling before opening their texts and began working on the first exercise, which was a fairly complex mineral formula involving percentages, oxides and oxygen numbers.

On his fairly large solid light brown wood teachers table were strewn a few daily business sections from an international newspaper, a few crinkled documents and a perfect diameter of coffee stain, left from his mug. The business section's headline caught his eye, it contained a huge caption, entitled - ViGnChi. What is next? - and pictures of - Vilmajev, Gunthar and Chiu. The article delved deep into the semantics of the Q90 deal, and that Gunthar would still be a heir to any changes, due to the contract with the Lornae administration.

Within a moment he turned to his class and with laughter said, "Class, that wraps up today's lesson, we'll expand further on it next class. For now, continue your readings and exercises, I'll be posting the assignment, due next month on the class website site. Please email me if you have any concerns. Continue reading the next two chapters, and I'll see you in two days. On an ending note, for those interested, we will be holding another -Protest - in front of the new ViChi office this Saturday at 2:00PM. Pass along the word."

The students all looked confused and slowly got out of their seats and proceeded out the door for a two day intermission of sorts. Some questioned why shift from traditional teaching method to the chalkboard and then call it the day. He hadn't done such a thing all semester, but now? Further, many students' questioned, why would Professor Dallas announce the planned 'Protest' in class?

Just then, the head of the school, Richard Sula was passing down the hall with Professor George Philipas, and noticed everyone leaving and the door open.

Looking towards the two approaching figures, he leaned to turn up the radio dial on his desk, which almost verbatim parroted the financial review piece on Vilmajev and Chiu heading in one path, while Gunthar and Gonsev to pursue path in defence and aerospace. Jason greeted both with a smile and chirpy, "Gentleman, nice to see you both again." He continued, "George, I hear you're heading to South Eastern next semester to head up the Physics department? As I recall, Sula taught there. Then again, so did my estranged parents. For a while, the present Minister of Economic Affairs, Milton Ferron and Mayor Joe Bohlm were my classmates. I did an Economics degree there first, before finding my true calling. South Eastern is also very close to the Epsilon 4 area and the indigenous regions."

George Philipas quickly acknowledged, "Yes it is. I'm going to miss you all, though new opportunities need to be explored. The Lornae administration has already spoken in many circles about advancing the pace towards future explorations there too."

That response lit Jason's eyes with disbelief, "Lornae is that quick. I mean even before going through the consensus, consultation, legislative and regulative channels? Wow, another sad hour unfolding. How about the indigenous communities and their land rights? Unbelievable."

"Now hold on Jason. Things maybe ahead of the curve, but by no stretch are they in any final phase. There are laws that need to be observed first, before the shovels begin any work there," Philipas countered back in a more diplomatic, and less terse tone.

Philipas then further expanded, "Over the past year, you all may have noticed that numerous foreign correspondents have been flocking to the Epsilon 4 and indigenous regions, almost by design, to promote a pure and future economic interest on the various global business shows. The tribal elders and chiefs are steadfast against it, as they have their ancestral land rights there. Lornae may be up to undermining them for a higher pursuit, I can't say for sure. This maybe part of Lornae's agenda, to advance his plans in increments. I have taken the position at South Eastern, but the Lornae Administration has also approached me about future, lucrative consulting work, which I still haven't given any signal of approval to."

"Don't betray your values my friend, and never sell your soul to the lowest bidder," Jason reminded George Philipas, while he shook his head in dismay.

Philipas then took a deep breath, before he looked Jason in the eyes and continued further, "Consortiums are already lining up, behind the scenes, for lucrative contracts, including Vilmajev, Chiu and Gunthar, who've already pitched Lornae with proposals. Many players want to explore, mine, extract and even build the Epsilon 4 and indigenous areas into another Bagerville within a few years. Massive resources of ores and precious metals are located there. You know what I'm talking about Jason, because you were there a few times."

Jason shook his head in acknowledgement, and with heartfelt emotion responded, "Yes, I was. I will organize protests against any development there too, just like I have in Bagerville, if I find any shred of monkey business. There is wealth there that would make Bagerville's value seem like a microcosm on a scale. If they develop those regions, in good spirit, and at natural pace, through the will of the people, only then will it succeed. There is a local legend shared by many of the indigenous tribal chiefs that, Epsilon 4 was created thousands of years ago, by a massive silver bird draped in flames that fell from the sky and made a nest in their mountains. Apparently only the initiated few were allowed near its nest to speak with the silver bird, and only the people from those regions are given blessings before the first seeds are planted in the spring, and in the fall, before the first crops are harvested. Whether that is myth, legend, fact or folklore, we must respect the indigenous areas and the peoples wishes that live there."

At this point, Richard Sula put the financial section of the newspaper on the desk, with the ViGnChi story, which by now didn't faze anyone, and only received a frown from Jason who begged the question, "I've already seen it, heard it and now see the same story before my eyes again. Is the Honeymoon finally over? Now more competition? Did we not touch upon and expand on this issue in detail last month at the Hemispheres Forum down south?"

The Hemispheres Forum was an annual panel discussion with global business, political and academic leaders, which dealt primarily with socio, economic and political challenges facing the nations in an era of constant change. President Lornae accompanied by a government delegation and academics: Jason Dallas, George Philipas and Richard Sula, flew down south to a resort like conference for the two day event, which was full of discussions and global signings on many fronts.

One of the key focal points of last month's forum was - Ethics and morals within a competitive environment. Jason was asked to speak at the forum, and did not hold back when it came to the need for more: accountability and transparency. At one point his microphone was cut short, some speculate deliberately to avoid embarrassment for the event. Jason barked at the Lornae administration, "You and your adherents have acquiesced to foreign demands for a major stake in a resource-rich area. You sold us out for chump change, and destroyed many family-run businesses in Bagerville, by expropriating their properties. These are people whose families have been in Bagerville for generations. You allowed for undemocratic forces to amend key legislations and regulations that make it possible for business to exploit economic interests without proper oversight. By doing that, it also enables funds to flow undetected in any direction globally, while at the same time evading our nation's tax system." Lornae tried to remain calm, though embarrassed at the event, but Jason wouldn't stop, he further countered, "Further to this is the lack of oversight, which makes it now possible for ViGnChi to exploit the workforce. Even further, they can manipulate the political and media establishment, and also make any product for sale globally, regardless of the moral or ethical dilemma it may create." Lornae was speechless, and refrained from making any comment, only slowly peering at Sula and Philipas, both were equally disturbed. The reporters from TV and radio were in a feeding frenzy with the news that was spewed out, and quickly regurgitated the news bits globally. Nonetheless, the return flight back to Bagerville was fairly silent, as Lornae wouldn't say a word to him, while Sula and Philipas remained quiet.

Shifting the conversation back to the present in Jason's classroom, Richard Sula who was in touch with both entities at Q90 and the government indicated, "The structure of the economic entities may change slightly, but we expect things to remain vibrant in Bagerville, as they work through the transition." Both George and Jason looked at him now with a puzzling look, while agreeing not to agree at that statement.

Richard Sula didn't stop there. In fact, he charged on, "I will support wholeheartedly all the efforts and be in the defence of continuing work at Q90 work. This split will now add a new layer of competitiveness." Jason just stared at Sula with a puzzling and perplexed look of disgust, before Sula continued, "The trade sectors and the manufacturing entities in the Q90 are said to also see significant increases in capital spending and possible increases in workforce, which will also positively affect Bagerville Polytechnic." Richard Sula then took a deep breath before examining Jason and George's faces. He paused still looking at both, before ending with a stark reminder, "Gentleman, whatever changes happen, the work at Q90 has become a necessary evil for the nation, Bagerville and especially Bagerville Polytechnic. We receive significant contributions, in forms of bursaries, grants and scholarships from Vilmajev, Chiu and Gunthar. They have created so many opportunities for our graduates, who don't have to leave the town to establish themselves, while at the same time build a more prosperous Bagerville, as it grows."

Richard Sula was still a spry and wise owl, and was keen on seeing that Bagerville Polytechnic received support from not only all levels of government, and also all areas of the private sector too. He met many times on private occasions with Vilmajev, Chiu and Gunthar, which he never fully disclosed, and some speculations only swirled that some favours and support may have been elicited. At many conferences, Vilmajev was always his strongest supporter, often stating, "The esteemed Richard Sula is a trusted voice and a beacon of enlightenment. ViGnChi will continue to support Bagerville Polytechnic, so that they remain on the cutting edge of education, while also creating more bursaries and scholarships."

A few days before, Richard Sula took it upon himself to ensure that the climate of economic confidence and stability in all political, economic and social spheres in Bagerville remained vibrant. He called Boris Vilmajev, "Boris, I would like to meet with you to discuss the changes, and the possible implications they may have for Bagerville Polytechnic and Bagerville as a whole."

Vilmajev agreed, and responded, "Mr. Sula, you are always welcome in my offices. Let's meet tomorrow, before noon, if possible here in my office."

The following day, Richard Sula drove towards the ViChi offices for a meeting with Vilmajev, when he noticed, Jason at a parking lot about 500 metres away. He was with a group of about a dozen people, and had his trunk open with some signage and placards inside. He was getting ready for another protest, this time near the ViChi offices, where Sula was going. Sula quickly parked his car in the visitor's area, away from view, then preceded to enter the building, and up to Vilmajev's office. Vilmajev and Sula spoke for about an hour, with both reaffirming their commitment to mutually support each other in many spheres. Sula let Vilmajev know, "I'm deeply concerned about the cleaving of paths and new entities being created. Are there going to be significant repercussions in Bagerville operations, Boris?

Vilmajev stood up for a moment, looking out his window, which overlooked Bagerville and noticed the protesters below, "Jason Dallas is back again today. This time with only a hand full of protesters below."

Sula just smirked, "Yes, he's very concerned, loud and passionate about Bagerville. Even when he was a student of mine, many years ago, he often showed strong emotions for Bagerville. His passions sometimes cloud his judgments. His philosophy is very nostalgic. A victim of progress at times, and a hostage to nostalgia. Every corner of the globe has a counter-reactionary movement. He is the backlash against the march of economic progress, which is de facto in Bagerville."

Vilmajev listened, and then proceeded to his vision, "Indeed he is. As for ViChi, you need not fear the split, Mr. Sula. I will continue to support Bagerville Polytechnic with increased funding. This we can outline further at a meeting, perhaps later in the week. Let's say at The Polytechnic. We should also have Lornae's people present, too. For now, I will directly tell you privately the following: a) I will continue to support Bagerville Polytechnic by myself if need be. I believe in the institutes of higher learning, and the tremendous work you and the other professors do there."

Vilmajev then moved his chair a little closer to Sula, took a sip of his bottled water and continued, "With demand exceeding supply, we expect to see significant workforce increases in many sectors. I cannot speak for Gunthar and Gonsev, as both are hoping to do more advanced manufacturing. I see more engineering and robotics there. Unfortunately they may scale back on employment there. Gunthar is more about efficiencies and the notion - 'more robots, less people.' As for Vichi, there may need to be some efficiencies at some divisions, but no major losses. In fact, increases in other divisions will offset any displacements. Chiu and me hope that highly specialized programs could be created in more - engineering, mining and robotics. ViChi needs qualified and knowledgeable employees. We see a massive need for more technology-based programs geared towards cutting-edge and innovative work. To aid in this endeavour, ViChi will be purchasing two units of each of its next capital orders for machinery and technology upgrades for retooling, with one of each item purchased going to Bagerville Polytechnic. These new technologies can be used as educational tools in your Technology and Trades departments."

At that point, Vilmajev stood up, looking through the window towards the Q90 area, then took another sip of his bottled water on the table and continued, "This gets me to: b) We would like to integrate the raw materials to the manufacturing process to run more efficiently, and reduce the times allocated for transportation. Both ViChi and Gunthar and Gonsev, will be making some requests in the near future to both

Bohlm and Lornae for a new high-speed rail link and highway. This could also connect, Bagerville with Ophidia, to the distribution channels, ports, rail yards and the airport too. A complete modernization of our infrastructure again. So, here we have more specialized engineering positions needed once again, as we hope to have this done in house, rather than through third-party contracts."

After hearing the positive reflection, Richard Sula became more at ease in his chair, and stated, "I will convene a meeting at The Bagerville Polytechnic soon, and request all of you to be present, along with Lornae, Bohlm and some academics. I will not mention a word of this meeting, it will forever remain between the two of us, here in this office."

Vilmajev agreed and then continued, "I will be there."

Back in Jason's class at Bagerville Polytechnic, Jason just stared at Richard Sula at this point and said, "Cannon fodder. We have become like vassals toiling on what is rightfully ours, while foreign hands pull the strings and call the shots. Our once great and proud agriculture and viticulture industries have been nearly decimated, and now almost all of them expropriated. Every request for a building permit gets expedited. The skyline in Bagerville has changed. We don't even have our annual Bagerville Harvest Fair, thanks to Bohlm. Of all people, he was what I considered, once a dear friend. We grew up together. Went through everything. Now, there seems to be an attempt to erase everything in this town's memory, for the sake of one or two economic entities."

At this point, Richard Sula felt insulted and lashed back, "Jason, the global economic crisis was severe. Clinging to nostalgia only enslaves you to a past, and never gives you the momentum to move forward. Your protests have fallen on deaf ears. There was no greater outcome that could have been achieved, to save the nation and the economy from sputtering into a dark abyss, where our GDP would have fallen by over 10%. I have convened a meeting with some government officials within the next few days, and would very much like you to attend, so that we can learn more about the impact any change may bring. Mr. Chiu and Mr. Gonsev have agreed to attend. The other two have declined. Minister Ferron is an old student of mine, when I taught economics at South Eastern."

Jason then began to chuckle and reminded Sula, "I remember. I was once a student of yours too."

The chat lasted another half hour, before once again, all agreed to disagree, while holding a consensus that they would have the meeting within the next few days at Bagerville Polytechnic to establish dialogue and forge a new path forward.

CHAPTER 7
SOLACE

Brushing its wings through crisp clear evening skies of only a few silhouetted clouds, one lonely brown hawk scavenges a sea of emptiness, while other birds hide from the predator in the lush forest of colours, near the farm fields. Some pigeons huddled together under an underpass in a deep corner, while some smaller birds nestled within branches and leaves to camouflage themselves. A few planes could be seen flying in the thirty thousand feet range, setting course for arrival, while the noise of traffic began to diminish. The autumnal procession of the sun was soon giving way to the moon, and its illuminating etches throughout the entire Bagerville escarpment, making way for a beautiful site.

"With a sunstone you could follow the suns path under any weather anomaly, yet with all the resources here, which are worth far more, I can't see a ray of light past those high peaks sometimes. How the hell did the Vikings see where they were going, when they sailed the seas, when we in Bagerville still don't know where we're headed?" Jason smirked, as he glided both his hands across the fence and railings of their backyard home. The directional compass of the nation was clearly not pointing to a certain future, when they gave away their treasures to foreign owners. Jason lamented to Gordana, "For centuries leaders in every nation on the planet showed bravery and resilience in the face of uncertainty. Yet it only took one economic downturn, to change the hearts and minds of our politicians, who buckled to fear, and handed over our sacred lands and treasures to the first group of conquerors for thank-you notes."

Jason and Gordana were about to sit down for a late evening BBQ of salmon and shrimp skewers, on their patio covered by a cedar pergola, and enjoy a few glasses of dry red wine, yet he was still being bothered by the day's events.

Jason only gently smiled at the fact it was a domestic Pinot Noir wine, and not a white wine, which he would normally adore with this dinner, both from one of the old Bagerville vineyards, now gone - Moltracheen Estates. It was a vineyard once owned by one of his closest friends growing up. When ViGnChi arrived, they squeezed the Moltracheen family out of their lands and vineyards. To this day, Jason always griped, "I'm sure Bohlm had a hand in it too. With friends like that, who needs enemies? The Moltracheen family had to sell everything, as the area and the surrounding land was needed for a ViGnChi sponsored infrastructure project - a new road." His friend Frank, used some of the money to open up - The Sundial. After going through that, Frank to this day has a sense of humour, in fact he jokes, "Jay, I still sell booze, even though I don't grow any grapes anymore." Deep down though, he knows the pain Frank and his family felt. He remembered as a kid riding his bike, with some friends by the Soma, near those small blue honeycomb-like vineyards all stretching on major trellis networks. Jason looked at the label again, and paused for a moment, when he read the date, "Gordana, this wine is from twenty-five years ago. A finely aged wine, from a once great Bagerville vineyard, that closed its doors over three years ago. Another industry in town, almost entirely decimated. When does the carnage of Bagerville's real industries end?"

After a few moments, he lifted the bottle firmly towards his chest and unplugged the cork, allowing his nasals to adore its scents for a few seconds, after which he slowly poured the wine into the glasses. With glass in hand, his thoughts for a moment began to drift to youthful days again. A day in Bagerville, when the fields were full of golden grains and crops.

His grandpa Jim was in the combine a few acres away, and he could still remember his laugh and tough words as he passed though the fields tilling and toiling from dusk to dawn, especially when he pulled out large pebbles and rocks from the soil. He tilled that land endlessly, like a comb passing through the soil removing rocks. Jason remembered a time when he was twelve, "I used to run through my Grandpa's fields, hands extended in the summer's sweltering heat and shine. I could feel the waist high wheat sheaves brush against my skin, while the smiling sun caressed me, with the clear skies above." Those one hundred acres of golden sheaves of Bagerville in the lower elevations, were always overshadowed by the unknown and untapped higher elevations in the Q90 area, above the Soma's edges.

He loved his grandpa Jim - he was always there for him, more than his parents, so his memories were strong. His grandfather raised him, as both his parents were also academics, more immersed within their own worlds, and constantly moving from one university to another in two continents. At the age of six, both his parents had no time for their only child, and literally abandoned Jason to the care of grandpa Jim, who gladly took him in, and raised him like a son. Jason never forgot, nor forgave the abandonment, and became very attached to his grandpa, and his love of Bagerville. At one point during his first years at South Eastern University, where both his parents taught - Jason communicated very little with them. In fact, he came back to Bagerville every weekend too, as his grandpa was always supportive of him and everything he did. Grandpa Jim also supported Jason after he did his Economics degree, after realizing his true calling was to be a Geologist, and go back to a university closer to Bagerville. The same could be said for his old friends, Ruddy, Frank and Joe, who were also always supportive, and also very attached to old Jim Dallas and the love of Bagerville.

Grandpa Jim told young Jason many times, many decades ago, "Jay, one day when you're older, they're gonna realize that the wealth in those mountains is more than the land down here is. When that day comes, it will change Bagerville forever. Greed will steamroll through our farmlands and vineyards and decimate this great place, all for the sake of a few coins. They'll even get rid of the annual fair. All the families of Bagerville will become just a distant memory, and nothing more. Don't let them do it, Jay, because when that day comes, greed will overpower this place, and when it does, everyone will turn on each other for a slice of the pie. Mark my words." To this day Jason still remembers those prophetic words and moments fondly, and the oath he gave his grandpa Jim, "Grandpa, I won't let you down."

When the events in Bagerville accelerated, Jason, Frank and a few other members of the Moltracheen, Zelk and Voss families, got together and convinced mayor Bohlm to attend a town hall meeting. Jason was overwhelmingly nominated to speak on behalf of Bagerville at the town hall, "Great people of Bagerville, I'm with you, more than you will ever know. We will fight this battle, through legal means, and through peaceful protests. We will resist non-violently and show them that this is our home, and respect must be earned and not purchased. We are here to send a verbal protest to Mayor Bohlm. We the people elected you, to look after our interests. Be our voice in this battle too, Joe. Don't turn your back on us." Jason remembered the cheering and clapping after his speech, from the many Bagerville townsfolk that quickly grew from dozens to hundreds.

Sadly, the sand and rocks on this earth remain far longer than we, and so too did his grandpa Jim leave this earth decades ago, and didn't get to see his prophecy come true. Now all that remains are great memories and words, while is his grandpa Jim is forever immortalized in a grey headstone. Jason took a deep inhale and smiled after that memorable moment about his grandpa Jim, that was etched within his conscience and focused back to the present, where his wife was seeing his focus and attention dissipate and then return, as if from a trance. Those three ring binder photo albums were also on the table, as Gordana brought them out earlier, and with the wine the memories came like a torrent as they flipped the pages. "Look at these great memories in these photo albums, Jason," Gordana began. She paused then continued, "Bagerville five years ago, ten years ago, twenty years ago. The family photos, including a few of Matt riding his bicycle. Here are a few more from the Geological Symposium overseas. Here's a picture from Matt's 10th Birthday party. These pictures always bring out so much joy, and sometimes a few tears."

Jason kept leafing through the pages, before she smiled, nodded her head, and said his name slowly, "Jason." She raised her wine glass, waiting to clang and toast. Jason finally closed the last photo album, aligned all of them on top of each other, smiled, clanged and said, "Memories always remain, but the future is where we are headed."

With a very rigorous day past: meetings all day and three classes to teach, Jason thought he'd better spend an enjoyable and stress-free evening with his wife. After dinner he could then resign to an easier escape and go to sleep, only to wake a few hours later and go through another mentally exhaustive journey at the Polytechnic. Again, Jason's thoughts drifted to memories of the past 24 hours. The chalkboard episode, and the brief meeting with colleague, professor George Philipas, who was leaving for a position at South Eastern, and head of the Polytechnic Richard Sula. They wanted to have a meeting at Bagerville Polytechnic with government officials within the coming days. He dreaded it. It kept running through his mind uneasily. Ever since ViGnChi effectively came and conquered Bagerville with their massive expansion, Jason was not the same. He felt it was too much power for one large entity. He also despised their tactics, particularly at the R&D lab. Furthering to his dismal outlook was the fact that Mayor Bohlm had no clue what was going on, nor did he care.

He always held to the belief that: absolute power corrupts. Clearing his mind a bit, he flipped the Barbeque lid open, fired up the cylinder and waited for the heat to hit three hundred plus degrees, before he was going to place the juicy and firm skewers, Gordana had marinated in olive oil, rosemary and lemon shards in the stone dish. She no longer taught, since she began to use an inhaler and have breathing episodes - now she was on a long-term disability leave. She loved teaching, but was advised to take a leave. Gordana found many new interests, as she would try to tend to their vegetable and rose gardens, while also finding time to read voraciously, books by the likes of: Tolstoy, Murakami and Ducic.

While the heat began to rise, the robust autumn scents and Soma filled the evening air, and blended finely with the two lanterns glowing with cinnamon candles in each corner of the patio. Hovering around the green shrubs and lighted fixtures in their neatly manicured yard were a few pesky mosquitoes and moths, passing every angle. Jason ducked and slapped a few off his arms, before squinting at his old injury that nudged him with an awkward pinch. After a slight sigh, he continued monitoring the skewers, that were basking in scents and searing, while Gordana set the tableware, plates and napkins.

A fresh multi-grain baguette was cut into pieces, and a bamboo salad bowl full of small and crispy cuts of romaine lettuce was also placed beside the wine bottle. Noticing all the placements, Jason, honed his attention on one thing only now, and with a grasp reached for the wine bottle again for a refill. After a few minutes he said, "These grilled champions are almost ready, give me another minute and then I'll slide them onto our plates." He then shut the BBQ lid again, and closed the propane knob. Jason and Gordana were finally going to sit down in their black cast-iron chairs, and begin to finally take their first bite, as they smiled at each other.

They raised and clinked their wine glasses, quickly scenting the flavour underneath their noses first, than pinching the stems underneath the bulbs stronger, looking and smiling at each other, while sipping slowly. A short wheeze caught Gordana, as she reached for her puffer that she quickly used to inhale deeply once before resting it down. A few of her fingers than began to comb through her hair, before she looked over to Jason and gave him another smile. A small breeze than passed, caressing their necks, while a small plane could be heard overheard leaving the airport, yet they still remained in silence smiling at each other.

"I was thinking of a Sabbatical," suddenly Jason blurted, with utter conviction. Gordana begged him to repeat it, "A what?" He smiled at her this time and confirmed it again by saying, "I need to take a Sabbatical. Time away. Away from this corrupt atmosphere. The area feels like it's been illegally annexed and plundered. Write a book. The two of us go and clear our minds. What do you think?" Gordana, still smiling and holding wineglass bulb within her palm now, slowly responded, "Jason, I think they need you too. We can go on a trip later next spring or even in the summer. Plus, Matt still has a few years left before he's on his own feet." Jason smiled, put one hand in his left front pocket, while with his right hand's index finger, he began to make circular motions, before he reminded Gordana, "Finger-painting. Remember Matt in grade one? We were downstairs near the fireplace, and he would finger-paint the Q90 mountains, the house and stick figures of the three of us. Time flies." A few small tears flowed down Gordana's cheeks, before she responded, "Time is precious, and it flies by. Almost twenty years have passed like a blink of an eye." Trying to change the topic, Jason snapped back with, "We'll have to do a weekend outing soon. Hiking, canoeing or cave exploring would be great. It would be nice to take that sixteen-foot fibreglass canoe out again, and slowly dip the paddle blades near the bow at 90 degrees, on the Soma and stare into the waters, and see the pike and trout dance beside the stern. Matt will join us." They both then smiled, while looking at their plates and drinks in front of them still.

The night was still young and all the day's events faded and the present was only the focus. With the weight of emotional pain, Jason looked her straight in the eyes and began with the day's painstaking events, before reducing the synopsis and saying, "I'll leave it for another time." Matt was out with his friends, so it was just Jason and Gordana at the table. The large dry red wine bottle was the centrepiece of the table, now only one quarter full. Their glasses clanged again, as both pairs of eyes met, before they each took a small sip and smiled. After a few seconds they placed their glasses down, and got up for a kiss and exchanged three amorous words, before continuing to enjoy their skewers, salad, baguette and more red wine. Rolling his eyes, Jason, sarcastically recited, "They. They. They."

CHAPTER 8
OPPOSITE DIRECTIONS

Large transport trucks heading down from the Q90 area, driven by fairly young Truckers, both having just completed a new seven week truck drivers course, only a few months ago at Bagerville Polytechnic, acquiring their licenses with air brake endorsements. Bob and Mark did the in-class and on the road training together, learning everything from driving in dry, wet and icy conditions on major roads and highways, to wide right turns and button-hook maneuvering. For last two-week interval, they were taught about the complexity of Bagerville's terrain, which encompassed the Q90 mines and industrial complexes, and how to shift gears correctly when hauling down long-winding stretches.

Further, the course also taught them on correctly connecting and disconnecting the couplers on the trailer, and loading and offloading techniques, which was all great to know. They both thought the course was detailed, yet they disliked the manual pump truck with pallets, boxes and barrels lesson they had to master, where they had to learn how to load correctly on the trailer.

Not bad for a well paying job for a couple of young lads starting out, now operating eighteen wheels, hauling tonnage for one of the Q90 logistics warehouses, burning large quantities of diesel. Now both were turning the wheel and changing gears, monitoring the CB radio chirping and snaking down the lower elevations, approaching the bridge over the Soma, for an early work detail.

The roads coiled and snaked, thus the name - Snake Valley. There the ground is darker, and the sky is grey from all the work related pollution, while most of the signage in the area is littered with orange pylons and construction signs.

Both of their instructions were clear, from a higher source, to take the contents to two locations and present the manifest and documentation. The authority and logistics behind the snake-like instructions, was also the mastermind behind this early morning run. Gunthar made a very important visit days before to the customs office and the forwarding company, discussing behind closed doors the terms of the final outcome and the script that was to be followed. He also made sure a shipping manager would do him an important favour.

Under the cloak of secrecy, Gunthar wanted to reassure himself, and two overseas defence contractors, who had some highly sensitive items manufactured to specifications at one of the GN-MG plants, that their items would arrive on time, and without any delays. Gunthar took it upon himself, to follow the entire supply chain process, "I need to double up on efforts, to ensure these goods are expedited with added measures."

The customs office staff were all ears, eyes and open hands to the envelopes that were received for their nod of approval, and silence in the project, as the deals cut behind closed doors were forever to remain unspoken. The documents were to be expedited, and everyone was to ensure that no problems arose.

The forwarding company was richly compensated for their documentation, which artificially left out a few digits, thus reclassifying the goods into other categories, while also stamping the certificate of origin, as authentic. Gunthar was elated, "Sometimes in life, you must reward obedience with monetary compensation," he would often state to those in his inner circles.

Sometimes the golden handshakes in business are a lot sweeter behind closed doors, when envelopes change hands, and winks are given. For some of the staff in customs, a couple drove to work in new cars the next day, another put down a new down-payment on a home, while a fourth booked a nice vacation at a five-star resort. Sometimes great things do come in small packages after all.

Back on the road, both trucks were heading closer to their destinations now, as one of the rigs radio's went off, "Come in Mark," chirped the CB radio, in the first transport truck. "Yeah go ahead," responded the young and eager buck, who was sailing and turning the wheel, while listening to some country music in the background. "Take the trailer," the rustling in the cab area and the rain coming down onto of the truck distorted the message, but the trucker got the gist. With all instructions, driving and full force concentration, his phone rang again. This time it was a text, from his girlfriend Sally. "Mark, I have two classes this morning. Lets meet later this afternoon in town, somewhere other than The Sundial, for a coffee. Oh, I forgot, you left the keys with Uncle Frank at The Sundial. I'll pickup your wheels after class for you. Drop me a quick line and let me know when you're done. Love, Sally." He got a smirk, after last night's intake of beer and pool at The Sundial, and focused back to driving his 53' trailer with 25 pallets.

The other trucker, Bob with the flatbed, pulled and forked in the opposite end, through the wet and gritty ground, heading for the rail yards terminal. He got a reminder about two minutes after, and responded back with a more protocol scripted, "Roger, I copy that." In the back of Bob's mind raced the notion of, "I want to get this work done, and get to the massage clinic, first thing after this shift." He was in some discomfort from a slight pinch nerve on his right side, and needed to see a massage therapist soon. At least a half hour before he left with his load, he attempted to quickly enter the cabin area, and lost his footing on a step towards the front of the truck. He tried to grab the driver's side mirror handle, and slipped a good few feet back to the side, before landing awkwardly on the ground. He felt the twitch, and muscle pinch, and it only got worse by the minute.

Within ten minutes, both arrived at their destinations, and presented all their documentation. The staff at the warehouses had further instructions for the containerization, consolidations and deconsolidating of cargo - heading to a international zones, where conflicts and tensions were brewing.

Almost a mirror image of the sound of air brakes releasing could be heard, before the ignition was shutoff, and the sound of doors shutting could be heard, at the two locations where the goods were being dropped off in their dock bays. Now both Mark and Bob, headed towards their respective departments to present their documents to other levels for these shipments. Everything was planned from a guiding hand, working the shipments in two directions.

In the background, a few forklift operators turned on their propane valves, and started heading to one of the arrived trailers, which were backed into the docks. The blue and red trailer couplers were still exhausting the air, while the two steel doors at the back opened emitting a creaking hinge sound, before the bulk cargo was revealed resting crated on pallets in boxes and nylon wrapping and straps with paperwork attached. A shipment for a defence contractor overseas, intricately designed, cut, fabricated, and ready to be assembled at another location for further use or market.

The cargo would need a further 24 to 48 hours for containerization in the warehouses, as one was headed to the port of Malmsburg, the other north east of the Himalayas. Once everything was ready, the next destination was going take the goods to the nearby port, where a crane, fitted with arm would lift the container, and place it on the vessel. The vessel was already docked at the quay awaiting the shipment for oceanic journey, to the northeast frontiers of another continent.

The intricate components were made in Bagerville from some of the finest alloys, unfortunately for some wrong reasons, but that didn't faze Gunthar one bit. He had all the money in the world - to him it was just a big arms race and chess game, steered on by his ego. Gunthar exuded an artificial smile, lacking in sincerity and honesty. Further his long gone vanity, was masked by his still arrogant and demeaning behaviour showing others - despite his blindness to his age, and leathery appearance, he felt that he was still above everyone.

All the customs offices and financial institutions involved with the transactions never questioned the authenticity of the documentation; they just passed everything through without question, sometimes adding a few items, for a few extra payments. For the next few projects, Gunthar would try to get Gonsev to sign off, as he felt he needed to focus his time and attention on bigger scenarios.

A few days before, Gunthar also made sure that two of the finest lads the shipping department could send, would do the special task of delivering the contents in two trailers, to two different directions. One of the shipping managers, Donny at Q90 gave Gunthar his solemn word, "The goods will be delivered on time, and at a very early hour, just as you instructed."

Gunthar then told Donny, "Seeing this is urgent, and done well, ensure that the boys be given the rest of the day off, after completing this important assignment."

The shipping manager Don, once again doubled down on his word, asserting, "I'll personally see to it that the cargo arrives super early Mr. Gunthar, and that your orders are carried through. I'll come in early and dispatch the information to Mark and Bob myself. Further, I'll make sure to give them the rest of the day off upon completion. If you have any questions, call me at the dispatch office tomorrow morning. Have a great day."

Back at their receptive drop off points, both received calls, one at the warehouses the other at the rail yards, this time not on their C.B., but on their cell phones. The mysterious voice asked mechanically, "Have you arrived?" and after hearing their responses only said, "Good. Enjoy the rest of day."

Both Mark and Bob felt like they had won the jackpot or a lottery, it was the easiest piece of work they had done in years, and they still had the rest of the rest of the day to do whatever they wanted. Mark had his mind set on hooking up with Sally earlier than expected, so he sent her a quick text message, while Bob immediately began to dial the therapist's office on his cell phone, so he could get the earliest appointment this morning.

CHAPTER 9
JASON AT THE POLYTECHNIC

It began to rain very hard the following day, as thick carpets of grey and pockets of blue clouds descended with a darkness draping the town. Early in the morning after preparing everything for the meeting, Jason left his abode, bundled up in his brown waterproof fall jacket, and his metallic hand lens magnifier. He carried his hand lens religiously around his neck on a leather lanyard, almost like a ritualistic amulet. It was still dark, with stars in the sky, and through the autumn damp and mist of the early hours, he went to start up his car enroute to the school, at least three to four hours earlier than the doors open.

He couldn't sleep the night before, so he got up early and drank two cups of aromatic Sumatra coffee, and ate a banana bran muffin. Gordana understood a lot was on his mind, and only winced, before asking, "I hope you left me some, as the coffee smells great. Call me later." Jason quietly turned to her, smiled and stated, "I'll call you later, as I have a busy day ahead. Go back to bed it's way too early."

As she slowly started to make her way back to their bedroom, Jason also began to quietly walk downstairs, and to the garage. Jason's scar on his leg from a many years ago began to bother him again, when he finally entered his car, he turned the ignition, and began to accelerate with slight pressure, while trying to focus and steer towards his destination. He knew the pain, reminiscent of arthritis in the rain, but he tried to shrug it off, making slight waves under his tan khakis he was wearing.

Over two decades ago, a blazing fire engulfed a school. He was nearby, when a chunk of smouldering steel came crashing down and jabbed into a few inches of his left Vastus Medialis, near his knee. The excruciating pain and subsequent recovery, still remind him daily, and serve as a constant reminder of fortitude, and its relation to the virtues of heroism.

He was much younger then, conducting some soil sample research for a project, when all of a sudden he started to sense dark, pungent burning odours in his nasals and throat, and the shadows of a moving reddish pyre in the making at a nearby school, reflecting off of his hand lens magnifier. Dropping his research equipment and tools, he ran towards the fire, where shouts, shrills, screams and distorted movements enveloped a school, where everyone, but one person remained trapped. Like a disjointed puzzle starting to unfold before him in rapid sequence, he ran to save the young, auburn haired lady in distress, who was feeling the affects of smoke inhalation very badly. He awoke with bandages wrapped around his leg at a hospital, almost twenty-four hours later. He remembers a much younger Dr. Rikaras beside him stating, "Jason, your knee should heal within a few months. You'll remain under my care for a few more days, before we send you home. In the meantime, I just want you to relax and take things slow. The recovery will take sometime." Rikaras then smiled, tapped his left shoulder twice as he congratulated him, before raising a newspaper up, and continuing, "You made it to the Bagerville daily - page two - with your heroic act. Look at that story and picture. They have you splashed in big letters - Bagerville Geologist Jason Dallas' heroic act of courage. This is worth framing."

Fighting danger with strength and courage, he was happy to hear that the person he pulled from the flames, fully recovered. Strangely through that act of courage, subsequent meet, the person he saved, would later become his wife, Gordana. At that time, she was a single, confident and educated woman, who had just started teaching at the nearby school, when through unfortunate circumstances they met.

Hands still behind the steering wheel, in the nine and three hold, his early morning reminiscing while off to the Polytechnic, was once again broken, by the jolt of two large tractor trailer transport trucks roaring, in the opposite lanes from a distance, heading towards the forks in the road.

The trucks were bending with the chevrons, coming down very fast from the higher elevations of one of Q90 zones, and across the bridge on the Soma River, towards unusual destinations. One of the tractor trailers, loaded to the gills coming from a manufacturing facility looked like it was heading towards Bagerville's vast expanse, away from the Bagerville airport cargo warehouses, the other a flatbed transport, with loads of strapped down contents, was heading to the rail yards for further transit to the east.

Jason's hands kept changing positions, from the ten and four, nine and three hold, while now perspiring and trying to figure out what the trucks were doing. His thoughts and his eyes scanned the two cargo carrying trucks loaded with goods, in the distance, knowing there maybe a 'sensitive contents' placard at the back. Mineral compositions kept racing through his mind over a periodic table on a chessboard, as to the character and shape that could have been in the back of those vehicles.

Jason began murmuring to himself, while turning down the radio volume, "Where are they going? The cargo warehouses don't open for a few more hours. Why are they driving down those roads that fast? What the?"

Through the distractions, he realized he now about four hundred metres from one of the Bagerville Polytechnic's security gatehouses to the parking lot B. Deep in his mind, he was hoping to do some early work, and a bit of research before the melee of morning began, at the ungodly hour of just after 5:00AM.

As he began to arrive towards the lot B, he swiped his faculty pass and the gate arm swung open. A faint and yawning voice came through the speaker by the gate-arm from security, "Good morning, Professor Dallas. A bit early this morning?" He slowly responded back, "Morning starts before the birds chirp sometimes, boys." He then continued slowly to sail his car into his designated spot, parking and exiting, before making his way towards the two large doors to the complex. He took a deep inhale of the fresh and fluid morning air, before tossing his car keys into his jacket, while tensing his leg, facial muscles and squinting with his eyes slowly. A leg cramp set in, so with a hop, he began limping on one leg for about ten seconds, before his circulation came back, and he proceeded down the path and laneway towards the concrete jungle of Bagerville Polytechnic. Within the back of his mind, amidst the cluster of all the daily activities planned for the day, he said to himself, "This is going to be a very long day."

A small four-door sedan with tinted windows had at least three shadowy figures watching his every move. Puffs of cigarette smoke plumed out of the rolled down windows. Eyes watched in silence, as the grey clouds began receding, and the rains began to diminish.

To the right of one of the figure seated in the driver seat was a burly character, with a laptop, which through the smoke, rain and mist could not be identified. The man without saying anything began to type some commands into his laptop, which quickly affected the CCTV, gate arms and some power within security office at the Polytechnic. After disabling some power to the security offices, one of the three men, calmly walked out of the car and said, "I will call you later with further instructions. For now, I'm going to the coffee shop. Now it's your turn. I believe you two know this building, and what to do?"

Bagerville Polytechnic's security had good old Dave and Allen working, sort of. They liked to mix leisure with work, while on duty, being on the internet or watching TV, while seldom going out for the walkabout on grounds with their flashlights.

Both were in their late thirties, and tipped the double-digit pound range, and were not interested in what they called, "unnecessary and frivolous exercise." Spread across their security desk were newspapers, an old pizza box, some empty cans of soda pop and keys to the entire Bagerville Polytechnic - including the keys to the security patrol car. The keys to the last item, were frequently used for runs to the local coffee shop, less than five minutes away - walking - and less than a minute away by driving.

Both Dave and Allen, were now comfortably reclining in their chairs, stretched out and catching some shut eye, not paying much detail to the security cameras that were frozen, or the signals that were out in the entire campus.

Someone spiked their coffees with a sleeping agent, at the coffee shop, where they had a box of donuts and coffees purchased for them by a strange, foreign accented burly man, said to them, "I have to compliment you two for the great work you do at The Bagerville Polytechnic. Here's a few coffee's and some donuts, on me." That burly man was a close, and trusted associate of Gunthar, who wanted to make sure that a couple of security staff would take a nap soon. Both Allen and Dave didn't mind the freebies, not knowing it was an elaborate plan to slowly sedate them for a few hours.

All cameras were frozen on a still-frame image of exactly 05:22AM. No staff, students or faculty were on the campus grounds, when the parked sedan, started up and slowly edged it's way into the parking lot.

By now, Jason was on the second floor heading for the department of geological sciences, to do some polarized light microscopy and analysis on some slides, before faculty and staff would start pouring in, and disturb him. He began thinking deeper about multiple issues, when some footsteps and rustling, setoff an uneasy sensation of fear to creep in behind him. As his shoes began to rhythmically rub and tick on the concrete and tiled sections of the floor, his sixth sense picked up some negative vibes. Hearing some noises, the vibes became stronger, and his heartbeat raised a few notches, before a bit of paranoia sneaked in, through the grey and soulless corridors. He took a few more steps, and that feeling began to creep in again, before he turned around and saw nothing. Then all of a sudden he heard, "Professor Dallas!" It was a vaguely familiar voice, which echoed from down the hall, but he couldn't make out who it was. He then stopped and squinted to the area the voice was coming from, before realizing, "Vlad? Is that you?" Then with a more of reassuring tone he stated, "Isn't it a tad early to be here Vlad?" Vlad also surprised, replied back, "Yeah, I'm working on a piece for the Bagerville Observer, and some other research work. I came in to do some work."

Vlad then continued, as he smiled and looked at his watch, "Some school work too. I'm planning on. Ah never mind. It's complicated. Too risky. Still in the early stages."

Jason emphatically responded back, "Matt mentioned something to me the other night. A piece on." He paused, let out an emotional tear, before he continued, "I'm sure it'll be very informative. If there is anything I can help you with, please let me know. One thing though Vlad, I want you to be careful and know there are powerful forces at play in this town now. Our protests have sent a clear message, but corruption is still rampant, and some of these individuals are more than just numismatic collectors of coins and currency. I hope one day the Voss family lands will be returned to you guys. Honour, pride and good judgment are sorely lacking. Trust is hard to find."

Vlad was in total agreement with that statement, and then revealed his belief, "My dad has written things off. He's very disappointed, broken and feels powerless about the way things have turned. But I actually think, there is hope. The protests you began are growing. There are more of us now willing to let our voices be heard." Without hesitation he continued to elaborate on some ideas and possibilities, before more footsteps and keys into the hallways could be heard, that they suspected was one of the security staff making its rounds.

For about two minutes, the two began exchanging some further detailed information, as they walked slowly down the halls.

"Mr. Dallas," Vlad began, before pausing a few seconds to collect his thoughts. He then continued, "Those mines in the Q90. They must be worth at least a hundred times the amount they were given to ViGnChi. That area is like a vast sea of resources for so many industries. It just baffles me. How on earth a nation could give up everything like that to a sole source entity and why?"

At that point, Jason Dallas just stood calmly in front of Vlad, looking at him and breaking a small smirk, before he simply stated, "Exactly Vlad. Exactly."

Vlad then continued delving on Q90, "Why the special economic zone and autonomous powers for the area? There has to be some element of corruption or higher interests. What do you think Professor Dallas? It's like one entity immersed in wealth and vanity, picking from low hanging fruit."

Jason kept nodding his head in agreement, and simply repeated, "Exactly. Vlad, I totally agree. There is no doubt many activities are questionable, yet the government has altered so much of the legislation and regulations that you have to ask why? In Bagerville we have almost become like serfs to a colonial master, while the mayor has become a pawn for them to use. This is a battle that must be fought on many fronts legally one day."

Then all of a sudden, within a moment of Jason's last comment, a clank and swoosh sound could be heard coming from the basement, as the entire power was cut, causing the backup generator to quickly kick in, before it too, gave off a horrendous wailing sound before losing power, causing complete darkness. The entire complex was now without a sliver of light in this dim hour, as even though the windows, the overcast skies shone no early ray of light that could seep into the Polytechnic's halls.

It became like night within the campus, very few items were visible and the illumination from a handful of objects only gave reflection to the walls and floors around them. Both looked at each other puzzled, before Jason asked, "What happened? Did we just get a blackout? Where is the backup generator now?"

Within seconds, heavy weighted stomping, moving in rapid motions were headed towards them, resembling a stampeding herd of cattle being let loose.

A silhouette of some monstrous figures, resembling individuals Vlad may have seen somewhere. The Sundial or somewhere else? The ones from the back table? They looked familiar. He was sure he saw them somewhere else. At this point, both Jason and Vlad simultaneously murmured, with all their facial muscles pulsating erratically, "What is this?

Like icicles probing and jabbing at open skin, the hovering dark shadows now circled around them, creating an ominous feeling through their veins and entire bodies. As they approached closer, Vlad recognized something on one of the monstrous silhouetted figures. The two figures, who were circling closer around them, were the same two at The Sundial a few nights ago.

Jason who couldn't see their faces, quickly and loudly yelled out, "What is this? What do you want?"

At that point, fear had overcome both Jason and Vlad, and their hearts were racing, muscles and limbs pulsating and perspiring from unknown figures encircling them in silence. "Silence is better than false theories, Mr. Dallas!" a rather gruff voice, enunciated ten syllables. Trembling with fear, Vlad and Jason, slowly pushed their sweat drenched backs against the concrete walls, while clenching their teeth and fists.

The thudding of heavy weight stomping on the floors, intensified, as they came closer, now a few feet away, though only a murky darkness could be seen. Then all of sudden, the sounds and fury of four fists, likes hooves of a beast, began pounding and punching, both Vlad and Jason with a tempo of a paddle oar hitting roaring waters. Warm beads of sweat mixed with the battering tide of quick cuts and bruises ensued, marking the targets with painful reminders.

One of the dark messengers grabbed Vlad, patting him down for any info, before screaming, "Your voice is way too loud. What is your intention?" Continuing, "You have drunk wine from a very deep well. What is it that you were attempting to find?" He then lifted him a foot off the ground, before thrusting him down with incredible force.

Shaking and trembling with major body aches, Vlad's mouth squeaked in a shrill voice, "I didn't do anything!"

Jason tried to intervene, but with a crackling of a fist to the lower jaw, he fell into an almost paralysed state on the ground. Vlad was then thrust one last time against the lockers, where his flesh and bones created a compacting sound.

As both lay on the ground, Vlad was quickly bound, gagged, and dragged on the floor, before being thrown over the shoulder of one of assailants like a lamb being led to a slaughter. Eyes flickering slowly, Jason lay fluttered on his side, as a callous figure moved closer to him, before punishing him with a few kicks to the head with his boots. The shadow above him spoke for the last time, "You speak too much Jason Dallas, yet you know too little." Eyes barely open and collapsing into an unconscious state, Jason faintly captured into his memory that voice and images of Vlad being whisked away, as he clutched his hand lens magnifier.

As Jason lay there, hopelessly moving his body around the floor, he could vaguely hear the school doors swoosh shut, and tires screeches from a distance in another area of the parking lot, where the campus-landscaping department kept their trucks and equipment. His peripheral vision was blurring, while he began to slowly fade into a helpless state that would last a few hours, before the campus staff would find him.

Struggling to lift himself off the ground and unto his one good knee and leg, their eerie voices and fists kept resonating in his mind. He tried desperately to reach into his jacket for his mobile phone for help, but his eyes slowly started closing, and his breathing started to decelerate, before he passed out.

Within a few hours, as the Polytechnic started coming back to life, the maintenance and security staff brought the power back up, and faculty and administration staff walked in to find him battered and sprawled on the floors. Calls for assistance were immediate and the response was quick and robust. Slowly awaking from what felt like a bad dream, with cuts, bruises and pain everywhere, Jason now opening his eyes, noticed familiar faces surrounding him this time. Sheriff Ruddy and the Polytechnics Richard Sula huddled around him, while a few paramedics were checking his vitals and asking him a few health related questions. They attempted to raise him up, before he yelled, "No, I can do it!" Everyone slowly backed away, as Jason slowly started regaining his equilibrium, like a newborn calf attempting to stand for the first time. As Jason got up, he looked over to Ruddy and asked, "What the hell happened?" Jason then cussed a few profanities and said very quietly, so Richard and Ruddy could hear, "I don't know! I don't know what happened or why? It was dark, and they kept repeating something. Now for the life of me, I can't remember, as it's a blur. They could be working for Gunthar, Gonsev or ViChi. I don't know. They rambled. Last thing I remember, they took Vlad!"

At this point, Ruddy grabbed his phone and called in to the division, and let out a final, "We're on it. We'll find him and we'll get down to the bottom of this, and quick." Richard Sula, visibly nervous began pinching with his right index finger and thumb against his blue necktie, signalling what some call a sign of distress, Jason didn't catch the sight, as he peaked at his cell, which had four missed calls now, from both Matt and Gordana. To his side, Ruddy by now was raising a brow, slightly twisting his neck to the right, and letting out a deep exhale of disgust.

"I think we have to have a chat soon, my dear friends. I believe there is something that you know, or may be reluctant to speak about, but I have to get down to the bottom of this. On top of that, an hour ago, we received reports about some odd tractor-trailer activities. Also a maintenance truck of sorts was ditched off to the side of the road near the Soma. That same truck was last seen near Bagerville Polytechnic before it went missing. Heck, it may have been Gonsev. I don't know!"

Both Richard and Jason's eyes met in a silent glance, before looking elsewhere, though Ruddy recognized with suspicion that a deeper involvement may be at hand. As the words became fewer, the stares became stronger, and the suspicions became wider. At this point, Jason's mobile phone rang again, and this time it was Matt. He answered the call trying to remain positive and yet somewhat elusive, but word broke somehow and Matt already had a view of the narrative.

"Dad, are you alright? I just got a few text messages from professor Tahlson and Bagerville Polytechnic's information technology department. Our classes have been cancelled this afternoon due to a security incident this morning, where a student and professor were roughed up. Everyone is tight lipped. What happened?" a slightly choppy voice asked, as Matt sensed an ominous force may have descended on his father.

"Everything is fine Matt. Things should be back to normal within a few hours. We'll talk later about it this evening. Can't talk right now," Jason quickly snapped back.

Matt just calmly listened to his dad, and the last few sentences, trying to piece together what exactly happened. His afternoon classes were cancelled, and there was some vigilant police presence in front of the campus. Further, the incident also made it quickly to a Bagerville news headline on TV, only vaguely characterizing the event as an incident involving unknown elements cutting power to the campus, roughing up a few faculty members, and that one student may be missing.

For almost five minutes the conversation delved further into myriads of tangents, before Matt finally mentioned that Gordana was on her way to see him at Bagerville Polytechnic, while he was gonna finish a few things first, and then head over. As the call ended, Jason's head shuddered with disillusionment, while seeking enlightenment in a vast sea of questions and suspicions.

CHAPTER 10
THE ART OF DECEPTION

Hours later, in the central nervous system for Q90 and ViGnChi, a phone rang three times, in one of the most influential offices, resembling the sounds of an old hand bell, where the individual behind the cold seat of authority was leafing through some recent purchase orders and schematics to a new work order. Gonsev left a few very important documents for Gunthar in his backyard. Within a short time, he was hoping to embark on launching a new organization, where he could mould the nucleus around the strength of an eagle's talon griping arrows, as opposed to handing out olive branches.

For now though, Thomar Gunthar wanted to keep his word and help those, with whom he had founded a global economic giant, transition to their new company, while also building his own. In his eyes, "I have already won!" He was part of an incredible deal, which not too many nations would acquiesce to, "I came to these shores, and I conquered. The next stage is more economic domination, to enrich my ego. I don't care about wealth anymore! I have more resources and value then some nations on this planet." Since his formative years, through to his rise in wealth and power, he became the antithesis of everything around him, empowered by the doctrines and philosophies of South Asian general - Sun Tzu - from over one thousand five hundred years before.

Thick layers of stern facial skin crackled, and both edges of his mouth began to pivot a mere ten degrees northward. Then Gunthar's eyebrows arched even further. An exhale and a tilt of his almost three-quarter century strong and solid neck, peering through the wrinkle resistant dark-grey conservative suit, caused another pop and crack sounding effect. His snake-like eyes blinked twice, before viciously snatching the phone, with his leathery right hand.

Preordained, at the exact time: 09:09AM, a gruff voice answered in a thick, foreign accent, "Speak!" Behind him on the wall was a large former ViGnChi logo, carved out of oak, and encased within a glass housing, as well as banners and logos around the room. The logo resembled - The Eagle of Lagash - the double-headed eagle. Yet this logo contained one dragon's head on the left, while on the right was an eagle's head. The outer ring of the logo was a serpent-like entity biting its own tail - the Ouroboros. Clinging to the talons of the half dragon and half eagle were the Cyrillic letters for "Vi" - resembling the letters - B and an inverted letter - N. Within the dragon's mouth was an East Asian logogram character for - Chi - while in the body of the Ouroboros, were two letters - GN.

Distorted crackling could be heard over the phone line, causing the voice to sound as if it was breaking up every two seconds, "Silence is better, but I fear that it was poorly executed. The message relayed, may have gone a step too far. Those two may be loud, but neither of them hacked into the system." The line started crackling again, as both voices just calmly pondered their next moves, as a certain incident was causing way too much attention for a small town.

"It seems there may be one more, but it may take time to find out who," continued the voice, which could not be recognized. The hacking breach really set the tone and pace to expand in many horizons immediately after Gunthar caught wind of it. He was determined that at any expense, he would see to it, without notifying the others involved, "Those responsible will be held accountable! I need eyes and ears in every corner of Bagerville to find out who was behind this hack. A message must be sent to the culprit, that this is unacceptable, and it won't be tolerated." As far as he was concerned, "A data breach, is more concerning to me, than loud voices and protests."

Thomar Gunthar was born nearly seven decades ago, in a remote village on the outskirts of a town near the North Sea. Raised into a poor family of farmers, the youngest of six children, since his early years he had to fend for himself. From an early age he vowed to rise from the ashes of poverty, and become more than mortal in every aspect, and not allow anything to stop him.

Up until he was twenty, he worked in mines, factories and even did arduous manual labour, eventually saving enough money to put himself through university a few years later. He eventually became an engineer at the age of twenty-eight, and worked on numerous projects, and was constantly rising through the ranks, yet always shy of becoming the main voice. Things changed about thirty years ago, when he launched a successful enterprise in exploring minerals, which helped him amass riches many people couldn't attain in a thousand life times. He had met Vilmajev and Chiu, through his various business travels and meetings, and the three clicked. When the golden opportunity posed itself in Bagerville, the three united and took the voyage. Since then, he has been on a path of pure lust for pitting opposing forces against each other, as a game, and nothing more.

Stretching within his dark-grey suit, Gunthar responded back with, "It is imperative that no traces were left, for anything but speculation, which can be countered with denial." The snake-eyed man in the suit continued further with, "There were two trucks filled with cargo, seen leaving this morning. Have you heard anything about it?" The other hesitantly responded back, "What cargo?" Gunthar than started to laugh, and changed the topic, "There are many new projects scheduled for the next few months, which will keep both Gonsev, and me, extremely busy. We're looking at creating at least two more advanced manufacturing, and robotic divisions in the near future. There are some trade shows overseas that I will be attending, and may require some of your services at. I will let you know the details at a later date."

Gunthar was speaking with a nameless close associate, with deep connections, who also arranged for a couple of shady characters to follow Professor Dallas and Vlad, and frighten them with a simple message. Apparently the messengers relayed something stronger, which was not the apparent intent. It appears that the messengers were concerned that Jason Dallas and Vlad, were attempting to have all operations shut down at Q90, which would have ruined the livelihoods of many, so they took matters into their own hands. They were now a possible liability, and perhaps needed to be dealt with too.

Many plans and meetings, raced through the snake-eyed man's mind, while still sitting in his office, so he decided to dial another number, to confirm if Gonsev was fully behind him in the new venture.

Mr. Mikhael Igor Gonsev worked on many global projects and designs, while also heading a few divisions of ViGnChi. He was well admired and respected for his knowledge, excellence and professionalism, and had numerous international contacts within the engineering and consulting world. Since the split, Gonsev was invited to a few international trade shows and missions, under a consultant contract accompanying Gunthar to explore potential opportunities.

As the number rang, a voice answered simply with, "Gonsev speaking." A detailed conversation began, with Gunthar attempting to double up on his attempts to persuade Gonsev to join him. After Gonsev earlier had called him and informed him about the hacking breach, Gunthar also knew right there that there was a high level of integrity in this character. With a sense of calm, and little emotion, Gunthar prodded him with, "Will you seize the opportunity?" He then continued, "Let your convictions drive you."

The solid mass of muscular flesh, who was recognizable by a slight graze on his left cheek from a battle, paused and reflected, before slowly responding, "I've given it a lot of thought, after coming to some of the trade shows and meetings, and my only price is of being an equal. Come to think of it, I have thought about it quite a bit, after our emails and chats. This new endeavour that we fashion from the ground up must be not only of success, trust and equality, but also one of ethical identity in every facet." He then flipped his sunglasses down from his head, to rest the arms around his temples and ears, and let the polarized lenses shade his always-alert eyes.

"It is done, as promised once before. Together, we will launch a new path together, though never cross me," sternly punctuated the snake-eyed man, while beginning to laugh. Gunthar had victoriously enlisted Gonsev, as equal within the new venture, where he wanted to stick to doing the deals, while he would let him handle the engineering end.

Gunthar also had something else in mind, that he would get him to sign off on most projects, some which he didn't truly want his name on, for various reasons. Gunthar dwelled on that thought a bit, before stating to himself, "He'll serve the purpose well."

Now reflecting, and posturing far more comfortably in the seat of his old office, Gunthar's thoughts went back to a meeting, that both he, and Vilmajev and Chiu had.

The direction of the compass was tilting too far to one side, while a third of the voices felt alienated. The pendulum had to be shifted quickly, and a cleaving away from the Trifecta, with a far more bolder vision and direction. This was always the ultimate goal anyway, but since arriving to Q90, Gunthar was uncomfortable in having ViGnChi feed the diverse, global: automotive, industrial, aviation, defence contractors and other disparate entities. His heart, mind and ego were bent on feeding two industries only, with mostly finished products that were high in demand. He only wanted to work with products that had - quality, a unique edge in precision, design and detail, which he felt he could corner the global markets in.

With decades of knowledge and experience in business, mining and engineering, he sought a skill-set, equal to being his right hand, that he could trust, and who equally held the same values of conquering and dominating markets. That person was Gonsev who had the code of ethics, experience and the education, to be his equal in the new venture.

Coded instructions from unseen guiding hands, pulling the strings and levers in a direction that veered in two opposing paths at times. Gunthar had his desires centred on satisfying his ego, "I have associates in every corner of the globe serving my every whim." After finishing his chat with Gonsev, he went into his computer, and looked up a few important dates in his itinerary, and the meetings he had with some important clients.

Four days ago, both he and Gonsev had met with Mr. Nakito Shungmei and Mhu Kei Tano, from Mei-Tan Contracting, a powerful defence contractor in the far east, at the an overseas annual - Global Aerospace and Defence Contractors Trade Show. Gonsev accompanied Gunthar to the trade show, where they had a booth set up, and met with many potential clients, exchanging information, while also putting together a dynamic video presentation of the Bagerville area and the Q90. Shungmei and Tano were impressed with the literature, and the video presentation at booth, and quickly agreed to meet within days to visit Bagerville and the Q90 facilities. Cunning, conniving and tactical, Gunthar decided to meet with the Mei-Tan officials without Gonsev, to secure a secret procurement of custom, engineered to specifications products for their assembly plant, after reassuring them that, "Concerns don't apply here. We are the masters of this domain."

Once again, Gunthar played the chess game - the money was nothing to him - the thrill was the chase. A deal was sealed, and the custom order was to be sent to one of the engineering departments. The work order was questionable, Gunthar knew this all along, yet he didn't care, and vowed to make sure it would be built and sent, no matter what. Once everything went through and the files were sent, Gunthar sent a quick email to both Shungmei and Tano, which read, "Mr. Shungmei and Mr. Tano, I trust your visit to Bagerville and Q90 plants was interesting. It's been a pleasure to begin doing business with you in such important capacities on this project. I will personally see to it, that it goes smoothly from start to finish, while also ensuring you that it will arrive in a timely manner. All the best, and I look forward to hearing from you soon. - Gunthar@GN-MG."

Also on his list was another client in the opposite ends of the globe, so Gunthar grabbed the phone again, and slowly dialled the number. He wanted to let an important client know that a shipment would soon be on its way on a container to a port, and that it would arrive within a month.

Reaching into his inside pocket of his sport jacket, a muscular left hand quickly snagged the ringing cell phone, while doubling up on the time, by looking at his highly luxurious, intricate and aesthetic watch from an alpine nation. He calmly answered, in his unique accent, while walking in an unknown direction, through an overseas assembling facility for highly specialized instruments, "This is Wilfstig. Go ahead."

"The documentation needed a few extra stamps of approval. No worries. It's all taken care of now. The shipment should arrive within the next thirty days," Gunthar began.

He paused for a moment, as the phone started breaking up, before he continued in detail, "The shipment will be housed within container number: Z5H34PL on the container ship, The North Doltmander which will arrive at the port of Malmsburg. Send the funds to the account."

Wilfstig responded, "I understand. Malmsburg. The North Doltmander. Container number: Z5H34PL. I'll monitor from here. Send to the account number? No worries. Thomar, can you send me the manifest, when you get a chance?"

Gunthar just smiled and reassured his client, "I already have. Check your email."

After the call ended, Wilfstig continued with his march to another department of the facility, while reading the contents within the manifest of the shipment on its way.

CHAPTER 11
FOUND

Vlad was found hours later, beaten and left for dead, clinging to the threads of life, near the town's cornfields. Nobody from the dozens of tractor trailers, trucks or cars that past that road way in the tumultuous past few hours noticed him, or even cared to stopped to see why the cornstalks were mangled, or the fact a body lay beside the side road. A couple of teenagers who were riding their mountain bikes, down one of the paths in the early morning hours did, when one stopped to take a drink from his water bottle, and heard a few murmurs of pain, coming from the mangled stalk and husks in cornfields. Immediately, one of them screamed to the other, "Call 911, and get an ambulance here quick. There's a body lying in the cornfields. Get someone here quick! I'm gonna check to see if he's still breathing."

Those that ditched him did so from the back of an old maintenance pickup truck used for landscaping, as they approached a rural road. The truck was loaded with rakes, trimmers and shovels, while Vlad was beaten and bound in the back of the truck bed, near the tailgate. No one even noticed.

The assailants threw Vlad out of the back of the truck, then drove over to a gas station, changed their clothes in the washroom, before one of them went into a phone booth and made a call. The gas stations surveillance cameras were rolling, catching everything including faces and the license plate of the truck, which they never thought about. One of Gunthar's close associates answered the call, "Ditch the truck somewhere near the Soma. Don't leave any traces behind. Those are your instructions."

The two were hired for cash, by one of Gunthar's unknown associates, who met them under a false pseudonym, leaving instructions, no names or connections. After the call ended, the associate noticed the number belonged to a gas station on the outskirts of Bagerville, so he called the gas station's manager. A sequence of dial tones were quickly tapped into the phone, before the mysterious voice began, "May I speak with the manager of the gas station. I have a very important inquiry." A male voice on the end of phone line quickly responded, "You have him. How can I help you?" Quick to concoct a story, the mysterious voice continued, "I just had one of my son's pass by your gas station with a friend, and wanted to surprise him with a video. Would I be able to purchase your store camera's videos for the past two hours? Lets just say I'm willing to pay a nice fee that will make your week's wages seem pale in comparison. Could I come in to speak with you in the next half-hour?" No alarm bells lit up, but the lucrative offer quickly made the manager begin pulling the tapes and respond, "Yeah sure. See you in bit." Gunthar's associate before disappearing back into the shadows, wanted to ensure that after he was finished with his services, and that absolutely not a speck was left behind.

A few officers from Bagerville Division 01 arrived on the scene, took notes from the witnesses and found Vlad - bruised and battered. One officer rushed out with a first aid kit from the car, the other immediately began radioing to the division and hospital for assistance. "This is car B-29, come in please. We got here before the ambulance," clicked one of the officers on scene, from the police radio.

Upon response from dispatch, he quickly continued, "We have a male, approx. age twenty to twenty-five. Semi-conscious, and breathing with difficulty. Vlad sustained large amounts of cuts, abrasions and bleeding to several areas of his body. Please send an ambulance to the outskirts of Rural Road 4. It's near the cornfields. This person needs medical assistance."

At the town's dispatch department, sheriff Ruddy was at his desk, going over notes, documents and some photos, and happened to hear the transmission, to which he responded on his hand held radio to dispatch, "Sheriff Ruddy, Division 01. This is Sheriff Ruddy, I copy that transmission too. Let me know when they arrive at the hospital. Out."

Ruddy pounded his fist at the table once, knocking some loose pens, and his cell phone to the floor, while his coffee mug barely fidgeted. He muttered to himself, "Jay. Bagerville Polytechnic, and now this! I'm glad they found him."

Vlad was grasping for air, feeling tremendous pain, and having difficulty every third or fourth breath. As soon as the ambulance arrived, one of the paramedics hoped out of the side door with equipment, and ran over to Vlad. He quickly placed an oxygen mask over his mouth and nose, checked his vitals and began resuscitating him. Vlad was then carefully placed on a stretcher, secured and placed with a blanket and pillow, and taken to a Bagerville hospital. As soon as the ambulance arrived at the hospital, he spent the next few hours in the emergency ward, before being placed in a quieter confine, to rest and stabilize. As he slowly awoke from his brutal ordeal, Vlad became more aware of the situation that had unfolded, after seeing the intravenous attached to his right arm, and the fluid to the side of his hospital bed on a pole.

The officers that were present continued their investigation, attempting to debrief him, yet Vlad fiercely and fearfully said nothing. All he kept repeating was, "Please – leave me alone. Those dark figures in this town will kill me."

Whatever happened, and who those dark figures that did a number on Vlad is a mystery – though speculation points to the some workers from Q90. Someone found something and gave him a warning. The next encounter wouldn't be so pleasant.

Passing the multitude of steel doors, hallways, rooms and multi-coloured lined floors at the hospital, Sheriff Ruddy Sark's weight and strength, moved in heavy measured paces of authority down the corridor towards Vlad's room. Authoritative, determined and deeply concerned, Ruddy had tucked under his right armpit some documents and photos, and in his left hand - his trademark coffee cup - always black, and no sugar or milk.

Dim lit room, with one lamp on, a nurse beside his table monitoring the intravenous and his vitals, there lay Vlad with a clean white sheet and blanket covering him. Still shaken, with some visible scars on his face and a few wounds, now cleaned with dressings and bandages, he quietly looked up towards the figure before him.

"We've questioned Jason, and have gone over other debriefing details. I have to tell you," Ruddy paused, before continuing. "I think there is more to it than meets the eye my friend. In my folder I have some photos, and some recent documents we've printed up from the Polytechnic's library with your name on it. After you were missing, we scoured all the surroundings for a clue. I began to dig deep. I think your beginning to see something. Hmm?"

Like two eggs thrown on the fry pan, the folder with some photos and documents emerged before Vlad's eyes on the hospital bed table. Slowly and carefully, while grimacing with pain, Vlad took the beds controller and slowly raised himself up a few notches to look and speak. As he notched himself up, one of the nurses in the room gave him a puzzling look, before leaving the room.

Vlad was parched, trembling and looking deep into what was on the table before him, before beginning to stutter as he looked at the Sheriff Ruddy beside him. Vlad looked very scared and continued stuttering, before Ruddy offered him a glass of water off of the table. Vlad snatched the glass with shaking hands, and sipped the water, like a person who had been in a desert for days.

After a minute, Vlad tried to calm himself down and began, "Mr. Dallas. The Polytechnic. Is he okay?" Ruddy nodded and simply stated, "He's fine. The good thing is you'll be fine too." Vlad at that point opened up and continued, "I. We. I found a few things. We uncovered something, but I'm afraid to say anything. I don't know for sure."

Ruddy grabbed some of the printouts he brought, and began pointing at them, "These files." Ruddy then paused for a moment, before continuing with his quest for more clarification regarding a document from Vlad's email account, "Can you tell me about these Vlad?"

Vlad nodded his head, while trying to avoid eye contact, and then responded, "I can only give you what I know. But I'm afraid. I think Matt something, or knows more."

A few more documents were then slowly placed on the table, the scene resembling almost a poker game. All hands were drawn, and awaiting the next card to fall. Grainy pixelated images showed a unknown burly character. This was retrieved and printed out from a mobile telephone. The burly character was wearing a black leather jacket, sitting with two other individuals at The Sundial – a person of interest to us, and part now part of the investigation.

Then a grainy photo of Gonsev emerged, at the side of a home with a knapsack, and something concealed in his hand, attempting to place something into an air conditioning unit or tampering with a gas-metre. Unsure what it may have been, it could have been documents that he was trying to leave in a safe place, but the home belonged to Mr. Thomar Gunthar.

Another partial printout emerged, a strange rendering or architectural draft with materials made from various alloys for advanced technological use in many industries. Only a few experts would know – Jason was one of them.

At that moment, Vlad's face became very clammy, his back was sweating profusely sticking to his gown, and he began hyperventilating again. He took one sigh and lost consciousness for fifteen seconds, before a female nurse ran with a stethoscope around her neck, after being called by Ruddy. She grabbed and placed an oxygen mask on his face and monitored his vitals, while he was emerging from the shock to normality again.

Within seconds, Ruddy kept prodding again with photos, "This man, he is a sort of jackal, a very bright, yet very questionable person. Known in the international circles as MIG, as in Mig Fighter jet. Mikhael Igor Gonsev. Tall, husky, with a scar on his left cheek - from a knife cut in one of those breakaway regional wars, some years ago. For an almost middle-aged man, he still prefers wearing combat pants that are snug. He'll wear deep green camouflage or black one day, then the next day a suit and tie. Damn smart too. He has a degree in engineering, a military background, and vast knowledge on information technology and programming. Built like an ingot of iron of muscle. Gonsev is a man hardened by battles, and loyal to very few. We've learnt recently, that he's been involved in some clandestine operations in numerous points in the world. Yet, he has immunity and passports from at least two powerful nations - all that vie him as their own. Protected from all levels of persecution. This brings us to: why is here in Bagerville? Why has he taken a position in engineering with ViGnChi? Is it money or is it a trophy of sorts to hang on a wall. Also, why was he in Mr. Gunthar's backyard? I don't get it! "

"The higher elevations in the Q90 area, and a new company that Gunthar and MIG are starting? There are some deep rumours about corruption on a large-scale. Our protests against Bagerville being exploited and corrupted maybe a reason that I'm here. I don't know for sure." Vlad blurted out.

"I think you know a lot more about these few items Vlad. Don't you?" Ruddy kept prodding further, while also in the back of his mind kept thinking of heading back to the division to do some further research.

Sensing a need to purge his emotions, Vlad looked at Ruddy and clearly and coherently mussed, "I think I know quite a bit about things at Q90, but nothing solid. There is someone else who may know even more," shaking and bowing his head, as if he was seeking penance before the sheriff. He ended his revelations with, "Sheriff Sark, I don't know what to say."

The conversation between the two didn't end, and in fact continued, and became quieter for a few more minutes, then Ruddy said, "If you remember anything, let us know." Ruddy then advised Vlad to get some rest, while he headed back to investigate some matters back at the station.

As Ruddy left the room, the nurse came in to check on Vlad, and noticed his exhaustive response and weak appetite, as his eyes were slowly fading into sleep, and only a few nibbles were taken from the sitting tray. Vlad once again tried to turn himself upright, before his muscles began to twitch, and his eyes fluttered a few more times, at which time he finally closed them for a few hours of rest, as he entered the realm of sleep.

CHAPTER 12
RECOVERY

Now restless, and recuperating from a traumatic ordeal, and chat with Sheriff Ruddy, Vlad was slowly waking from a nap, gazing at the ceiling, the window and floors, while countless questions kept racing through his head. A tray of food was still to his side on a table, he hardly touched it, while the glass of apple juice only had a few drops left. His ears were tuning into some intravenous and feeder noise and some beeps coming from someone on a respirator across the hall. At that moment he came to a quick realization that less than a few days ago, he did not for a moment think he would be in a gown in hospital bed, at Bagerville Hospital.

He quickly moved his eyes to scan for his personal belongings, as some of the pain medication was now starting to wear off, and he was more cognizant of the ordeal he went through. At this point he noticed he had a phone next to the tray of food, but he didn't have the energy to grab it, and dial home or call anyone. He grabbed the glass of apple juice, and absorbed the last few drops. He immediately felt a tad more hydrated, as his tongue and throat were parched, as if it were a hollow sand paper roll. He lost track of time. He wasn't sure now what day it was. A collage of photos raced through his mind - his parents, school, some writing he had to do, and then he closed his eyes to let a few tears out slowly. He shook his head and begged the universe for answers, as to, "What the hell happened, and why?"

After a few minutes of reflection, he turned his head to smile at the noon crack of light beaming through his drab window, while in one of his ears he could hear the floors squeaking, and some familiar voices approaching. He took a second peak at the window, seeing the Q90 mines in the distance, while also seeing a partial reflection of himself in it. He kept staring for a few more moments, and noticed his few facial scars now were a little smaller and dryer, after which he winced at the sores, gauze and dressings in different points of his mid section.

He took a deep breath while wincing again, while inquisitively scanning his area, before he began to slowly adjust himself with the controller. He fidgeted with the controller a bit more, before he was finally resting upright, which allowed him to finally crack a smile and open eyes a tad wider to the room, and his new surroundings. His hearing sensed the footsteps again, this time outside of his open doorway.

The first person to enter was a physician, who asked for a few moments to speak with Vlad, before the other two would enter.

"Looks like you had a pretty rough ordeal, Vlad, " he began, before smiling and continuing in a more nuance tone, "But you're gonna a make a full recovery. You have some abrasions, cuts and bruises that will heal within a week or two. No major concerns. Get plenty of rest; you'll be out of here tomorrow. Give my regards to your parents." Vlad nodded, and then squinted to double- check his identification tag around his neck, that was being obscured by his stethoscope. Dr. Mike Rikaras, who noticed and smiled, before telling him, "Vlad, I'm going to draw up a prescription of 50 mg of anti-inflammatory medication and some Tylenol for you. You'll take that to the pharmacy when you leave."

Vlad, once again nodded, as the Dr. Rikaras quickly scribbled down a prescription on a small piece of white stationary and then signed it. As soon as the piece of paper was handed to him, the doctor and his clipboard made his way out of the room, on his next round to other patients in the floor, before stopping just outside of the doors to speak with one of two other figures approaching.

"Dr. Rikaras? " a startled Matt began. The now slightly greyer Dr. Rikaras, extended his hand to Matt, before responding, "Vlad's gonna be fine. A bit shaken and roughed up, but he's going to be fine in a few days. Are you alright? Your dad, is he alright? Many years ago, when I was a much younger physician, I tended to Jason's knee. It was just after the Bagerville Fair, over two decades ago."

"I'm o.k. Dad's a bit shaken I'm sure, but still ticking. Me and Tim caught wind and rushed to get here," Matt quickly revealed, before continuing, "I remember on many occasions my dad fondly praising you as the Bagerville healer." Matt then paused and looked at Tim, before glancing towards the Vlad's room, one once again at Dr. Rikaras, before he diced his words painfully, "Now this. Dr. Rikaras. I don't know what to say."

Rikaras smiled, before stating, "It'll be alright. Send my regards to Jason and your mother. You two should go in, as I have to continue with my rounds."

At that point, both Matt and Vlad simply stated in unison, "Thank you, Dr. Rikaras."

Back inside the room, Vlad squinted a few times, as the two voices now became clearer and louder as they got closer to his bedside, helping to rejuvenate his moment of weakness. It was Matt and Tim, approaching with one of the nurses, who looked at him with concern, when they saw their pal laying there, in a gown with scars and dressings.

"We got here as quick as we could. Your parents are also on their way up. They heard you're alright, and figured you get a bit of rest," began Matt, while both nodded and gave Vlad brotherly handshakes. "No flowers. But we brought you some real food, and a real coffee," Tim added, with a bit of tongue and cheek comment. This caused a few chuckles, including one from the nurse that was just leaving the room, with his barely eaten lunch tray.

Looking at his friends directly, an emotionally broken Vlad began, "I feel mangled, though not broken. I feel ashamed, angry, scared and confused. I don't know who did this to me, and your dad. It was dark and quick. It may have been somebody from The Sundial. I don't know for sure. Maybe somebody in town is angry at our protests. Everything is still hazy. I have no proof. I don't know. How is your dad?"

Matt just nodded, before he scanned the room and hallway, before he quietly dealt his cards on the table, and revealed more information regarding his suspicions, and some further details as to the next steps that would be taken to expose all work at Q90. Within the silence of the three of them huddled, Matt said, "I will continue data digging further.

For now, I'm heading over to see my dad, and spend a few moments with him too." Tim deciphered his methodology quickly, and added, "I'll see what I can find within the vaults too, on my end at the bank, as I have access to many files on some of their past contracts. There maybe something in there." Vlad just intuitively sat there listening, and finally said, "A story will come out of this one day. A major story will come out of this. That I promise."

For nearly an hour the three coalesced around many ideas, before Matt came up with a unifying vision, "Guys, we need to expose all dealings to the police and media, in hopes of creating enough strength and momentum to awaken and shame the government into renegotiating the terms of the deal. Bagerville needs to retain a much larger share of revenues, while also having more oversight on all import and export activities passing through our doors. Vilmajev, Chiu and Gunthar have been successful so far in deceiving, evading and using Bagerville as a shell game. Our protests have done very little to raise awareness, so we have to up the ante." After their chat, both Matt and Tim before leaving told Vlad, "We'll see you soon. Get some rest buddy."

As Matt and Tim left the room, Vlad, experienced a new jolt of adrenaline, as he got up and stood up from his bed for a stretch, against the advice of the now present nurse. He felt an uncontrollable burst of strength, not only physically, but also emotionally and mentally, before he smiled and told the nurse, "I may fall, but I will always get up, and bounce back even stronger."

CHAPTER 13
A WAR OF WORDS

The die was cut and cast, as the meeting at Bagerville Polytechnic, was fashioned from a desire to coalesce around new opportunities for the area, rather than wallow in the sombre reminder of the reduced sovereignty over the area to foreign economic entities.

Reduced direct government authority in Bagerville, cascaded by a farcical mirage of full accountability and transparency, gave sway to many dark moments in the area. A monetary coercion now spoke louder than loyalty, and corrupt behaviour was always merely frowned upon and accepted.

The enormous resources in Q90, and the massive investments made in multiple operations to mine, extract and even process the materials into finished custom and engineered to specifications products, bore the stamp and seal of the nation and Bagerville. On the positive front, more intricate components for the auto industries made their way to many corners of the globe, and so too did various medical, surgical equipment and instruments for various hospitals and health-care institutions.

Adding another layer of questionability now in the Q90, was a shift in some plants to focus on the aerospace and defence sectors nationally and globally, without proper oversight. These activities raised more suspicions, and garnered more rumours that, "Bagerville maybe indirectly aiding military build-ups, and sales to rogue elements with no ties to a state."

At any cost, many in Bagerville and the nation, on the political, economic and even the academic front, wanted to maintain the status quo at minimum. Some even feared a return to the past would unleash cataclysmic forces that would damage many sectors of the nation's economy.

A few days ago, in Jason's class, the head of Bagerville's Polytechnic spoke at lengths about, "A necessary evil," which caused many disagreements and some heated discussions. In light of the rapid changes that were evolving within Bagerville and at Q90, President Richard Sula, set-up a closed door meeting with some academics, politicians and some leaders of the two new entities, which were to take place at the Bagerville Polytechnic. Also invited to the event were a few media representatives, and Sheriff Ruddy - though not in the official capacity, but as a private citizen - partly due to links to the community and deep friendships.

As many events evolved rapidly, so too did an incident with Jason and Vlad, and a breach of documents from both ViChi and new GN-MG operations, which were still on Ruddy's mind. He was not only deeply immersed in the puzzle, but also entrenched within a circle of figures from all walks of life in the town, some, who may have seen or heard something. His main goal was to attend, listen and possibly gather any clues, though in silence.

While entering the meeting, many warmly greeted Jason with handshakes, smiles and encouraging words, after hearing about his incident a few days ago. An investigation was ongoing, and still not resolved. Too few clues, and too many questions still.

The hope of this meeting was for a precipice of change, and to forge a new path forwards, while also seeking to find answers to some recent incidents.

Last minute, Boris Vilmajev decided to accept the invite, though Thomar Gunthar declined, almost sneering arrogantly down at the invite, as he already etched many new deals, and behind the scenes had total support from the Mayor Bohlm, President Lornae and his entire government. As far as Gunthar was concerned, Lornae gave him his word in Bagerville a few months ago, "I will back any change that may be decided upon, provided that investments and projects continue to move forward, and there is a semblance of growth, rather than stagnation." Gunthar and Gonsev's new GN-MG entity was moving forward, while some plants were being upgraded, retooled and refurbished with new investments. As far as Gunthar was concerned, his autograph was still a signatory - since day one, and any changes within the confines of the agreement stood. As for the meeting, Gunthar sneered at Vilmajev earlier, "Are you mad? What has come over you? You're going to support The Polytechnic with equipment and more funds?"

Vilmajev was more cordial, "Gunthar, I'm going to the meeting. Sometimes in life you give back. It's called giving back - Philanthropy."

Gunthar just continued with his arrogance, "Hogwash. Take no prisoners, Vilmajev. You are the master of your house, not Bagerville or Ophidia! Plus, Dallas will be a nuisance again."

Vilmajev then stated, "We maybe today's voice, but bright minds come out of Bagerville Polytechnic, and they will be tomorrow's voice one day. Education has always been an investment."

During the meeting at the Bagerville Polytechnic, Gonsev in order to not cause friction, distanced himself from Vilmajev and Chiu, and only politely nodded to them, as some wounds were fresh and would take time to heal. Vilmajev just stood still in his blue suit, with a beer in hand, and looked away as Gonsev passed by him, without a single word.

As Gonsev passed Jason Dallas, he extended his hand, which caused Ruddy to look over his way, "Mr. Dallas, I recently learnt of your misfortune. I hope you're doing better. I hope they catch those culprits. I must also say, that I truly admire the work you do. I've even taken the liberty to read some of your published articles on some geological surveys you did. I would very much like to meet with sometime, at your convenience to speak with you about the specificities of Titanium in particular."

Jason shook his hand, while eyeing him and responded with a sarcastic, "We could also talk about Tungsten and Palladium too. We could also talk about their uses, after the manufactured process. Their values and not just in the anatomical senses. By the way, where is Mr. Gunthar?"

Gonsev decided to take one step back and counter with, "Mr. Dallas, I hope I did not offend you. I was merely attempting to get your professional opinion. As for Gunthar, you may have to ask him yourself, the next time you see him, as to why he didn't come."

At that point, Jason lowered his personal shield, and realized that although Gonsev may have a deep history, but he most likely didn't have a role in the incident. After taking a view of the room, Jason simply nodded his head while tinkering with his hand lens, and responded back with, "We'll find an opportunity to speak at another time. As for Gunthar, we spoke about too many things already."

Gonsev then politely smiled, walked over to another corner of the hall to get a refreshment, and find a seat.

A few days ago, Jason was in one of the old areas of downtown Bagerville, when he noticed some old historic buildings had already been levelled, and signage indicated a property redevelopment with new zoning information. Beside the wreckage were skids of bricks, blocks, steel beams and prefabricated walls. Scaffolding was already getting set up about 10 feet away for this fairly large project. Jason began to seethe as he saw, Gunthar there with a hardhat on along with some contractors, while Yan Chiu sat in his car on his mobile phone. Before walking over to Gunthar and Chiu, Jason called Mayor Bohlm on his mobile, "Joe, what are you doing? I'm in front of some of the old torn down historic buildings near the downtown core. What happened? How could you tear down historic buildings in our town that quickly? Are there not any rules that have to be followed regarding, regulations, laws and zoning issues, some which can take months to clear? We're going to have less mom and pop shops and more big box stores now everywhere. The skyline is going to change. Why are you on a path to destroy this town?"

Joe just listened and snapped back, "Hold on Jason. These are all valid. They have permits. These are redevelopment deals for the area. The population is growing in this town, and we need to keep up with the demand for everything."

Jason just closed his eyes and hung up the phone on Joe, and then walked over to Gunthar.

Jason quickly drew Gunthar's attention and began, "Can there be a balance between progress, and respect for cultural heritage in Bagerville, Thomar?"

Gunthar just frowned at Jason and responded, "We need more space for industrial use in this area. Chiu is also looking at building a mixed commercial and residential complex beside us as well. Bohlm was kind enough to expedite the documentation necessary for both projects."

Jason just quietly looked at the construction project and Gunthar and simply said, "I hope you have a nice day." Jason then turned around and walked back towards his car, and drove back to his home with a deep feeling of sorrow for destruction of landmarks that were now present in many points in Bagerville.

Yan Chiu with his wife Jia-Li, made their way in, and greeted Jason and Richard Sula, and exchanged a few words, before proceeding to get themselves refreshments from one of the tables set up. While near the table, Yan Chiu took in a wide view of his surroundings, and noticed that President Lornae and Minister Ferron from the government were present. He also gave a quick nod over to Vilmajev that he would come over to chat with him later.

Enormous greed seeped through the veins of the conquerors from across the ocean, whose lust for more resources would not rest after hearing of new reports that new ground penetrating radar imagery had identified far more riches under the Epsilon 4 area than first imagined. Chiu was the first to seek a few words with Lornae, about ViChi interests in developing the Epsilon 4 area. Lornae motioned Chiu over to a quiet corner and quietly stated, "Yan, there are still enormous legal hurdles preventing any tangible exploration, mining and manufacturing in the area. This conversation may have to wait for another day. The entire area has vast potential due to it not being thoroughly explored, due to the laws governing the protected indigenous region nearby. Recently we had some drone missions over the area, and some vague satellite imagery, which indicated possible, nickel, zinc and chromium deposits. There is one person, Jason Dallas, who has been there on many occasions and knows the terrain and deposits. Good luck if you think you can get him on your side though."

Entering the meeting were also some quiet scholarly academics, scientists, some other low-key government ministers, and a few media representatives covering the event. The meeting was filling up quick.

Richard Sula began, "Thank you for all coming," as he scanned the room, he noticed, one person was missing - Thomar Gunthar. Continuing he added, "I have convened this meeting in hopes of getting everyone to unite and forge a new path moving forward for Bagerville, in light of the split within ViGnChi." This aroused a few smirks, nods and silent gestures from everyone, while Vilmajev, Chiu and Gonsev in attendance would only smile and not look at each other.

Vilmajev then got up, and decided to reassure the attendees on ViChi operations, by earnestly speaking. He began, "Thank you for convening this meeting Mr. Sula. ViChi will continue to build on our common goals and foundations, and strengthen our strategic partnerships. We want to improve all relations in every strata of society, and a recent data breach and hack solidifies it. Bagerville is home to a wonderful institution. A multi-disciplinary educational institution, that has given us some of the world's brightest minds, and a highly educated workforce. Resources, strong infrastructure, telecommunications, which have made for tremendous economies of scale." He then paused on the last word, and repeated it, before restating a breach that had occurred, and an investigation that was on going.

From the back, Ruddy overhead that key words – breach and hack – and scribbled down a few notes. Gonsev stood attentively clapping at the speech, while also taking note of the breach mention, and looked on into the crowd to see if there was any reaction. Once again, Vilmajev continued and went at depths about vertical integration, free-trade agreements and reduced taxes, duties and tariffs on all products coming in and leaving Bagerville.

Many began to applaud and clap for about a minute, before he continued his lengthy speech, "We want improved relations, to increase the standard of living everywhere and share in the prosperity. Spread wealth. We realize that we are here on this planet only so long, and you can't take all the riches with you when you go. I also want to highlight a recent two-day trade mission that President Lornae, Minister Ferron, Mr. Chiu and me attended overseas. A global medical device trade show, where ViChi had an exhibit, that many physicians, surgeons and dentists attended from various global hospitals, health-care institutions and dental associations. We showcased some of our highly advanced precision manufacturing capabilities, and were able to secure great contracts for some of our precision medical instrument manufacturing division, which will see a rise in output in all sectors within the coming months."

Vilmajev then paused, took a drink of water, before continuing again, "When anyone mentions - Bagerville Titanium - a resource very bountiful here, the results can be seen in the amazing knee and hip implants, articulating plates and sockets we manufacture here. We make these wonderful items, to exact specifications for the countless muskoskeletal and orthopaedic needs in every corner of this planet. In ending, the trade show, which was sponsored by various global aid organizations succeeded in bringing together business and health-care professionals under one umbrella at the show, where the mechanisms to aid in the modernizing, equipping and transforming the quality of life and healthcare in vastly under developed regions of the world were sealed. With the various global aid organizations absorbing 70% of the cost of the procurements for the modernizations, pending their nations and healthcare, hospital and dental associations approvals, the contracts were not only abundant, but were a sure sign of great times ahead for this country, and Bagerville in particular."

Jason was standing with his hands crossed and rolling his eyes, which was noticed by a few in attendance, yet not a word was said. Within a minute, triumphant clapping and thunderous applauses could be heard, before a microphone fell to the floor causing a short audible malfunction.

Within in minute, after the microphone was placed back in its spot, more applause ensued, this time for about two minutes, as more people began to slowly pour into the meeting. At this point, Vilmajev began to clap too, and even smile, before repositioning his firm stance with a few last words, "When you build bridges, you don't need to build walls of any kind. I believe in investment and growth, but I also believe in trust and rewarding everyone equally."

Gonsev looked over silently and felt the context may have been geared towards his direction, after the resignation and chat he had with Vilmajev, who seems to have felt betrayed by him.

Continuing to feed into the positive narrative of Bagerville, one of the governments dignitaries present, Milton Ferron from the Ministry of Economic Affairs, cut in with a diatribe, "Our strategic goals are: i) Reduce trade barriers, including all duties and tariffs ii) Open doors to further trade in all spheres iii) Increase economic growth and iv) Raise the GDP annually by an average of 3%, or better. These efforts will bring untold prosperity and renewal in all areas of the country, particularly if we can exceed the 4% threshold, and actually achieve higher than 5% growth in some quarters."

A few more applauses ensued, for at least a moment with many in attendance welcoming the encouraging words from some of the top brass of the nation, while Professor Dallas just ripped into laugher while glancing at a text message he had just received from his wife Gordana, it read: "I hope you're having fun."

After the applause ended, Jason Dallas could not contain himself any longer and finally barked out his emotions clearly, "Gentleman, I am not comfortable with all the Machiavellian activities taking place in our midst. Further, the leader of our great nation is only half present here, so he lets one of his emissaries to speak. This is beyond the pale. There are many questionable issues that have to be brought up on how to better regulate this wild west expansion. Things have to be brought to order in our own house. There is virtually no competition within this realm; our ancestral lands are being expropriated at a rapid pace. Your version of vertical integration is what I call - oligopoly! In short, there is an enormous erosion of confidence with everything happening, and we need to clear the air."

Further wound up, Jason continued with a scathing and unremorseful, "With all due respect minister, that sounds too trite. What we have here is perhaps national strategic assets handed to foreign hands on a gold platter for peanuts. We gave away massive reserves of Titanium, Palladium, Tungsten and other jewels! You guys gave away incalculable treasures to foreign entities, while retaining only a small percentage of ownership. How are they getting all the export permits? Are they altering the customs codes? How do they classify the materials? I have analyzed many of those resources and minerals under a Petrographic microscope for years, with countless individuals and officials, which concluded that these were - strategic state assets. With my hand lens magnifier on my lanyard, I was deep within hundreds of feet, in many of those mines and veins. I was there with my crack hammer, note pad and 250 lumens flashlight in the many times. With all the GPS surveys and topographic maps available, how is this possible? These are valuable resources. Is customs aiding them? Now that Gunthar is out, Vilmajev and Chiu only care about money and power, everything else is a facade. I would not be too surprised if you guys also gave them the Epsilon 4 area next. I don't buy the polished speeches, and I will not be intimidated by anyone. Within the past few days, the unknown has ruffed me up in this institute, and I'm still ticking. This gets me to the point, of Gunthar. He wants more. I think he wants to dominate some of our resources to feed the global military economic engines, as some kind of game of sorts. What did they pay you guys, Ferron? I will fight for Bagerville's interests and our lands, until the end, even if it's a battle of David versus Goliath."

The night before on an overseas news channel, a reporter proclaimed, "International defence spending has increased in many nations, while many conflicts are brewing in many corners of the globe. National military build ups are happening, while there is major muscle flexing by some superpowers, causing economic jitters, friction on the global stage and artificially inflating GDP rises in some statistics globally. Bagerville is said to be a major contributor to these military engines globally, providing many raw materials, if not even the components themselves."

Many in attendance viewed that news clip, because it also mentioned Bagerville, as a major source purported to be feeding the engines of some of these corners of the globe, where there were significant military build-ups, particularly in the aerospace area. President Lornae and Minister of Defence Pucitt, were clearly disturbed by the news, and intelligence briefings, and decided that to water down the story, an economic official should go to Bagerville for the meeting. The story was enough for President Lornae to quickly get on the horn with Ferron last night, who was also old friend with the town's mayor Bohlm, "Milt, I think you better head over to Bagerville for that meeting tomorrow." Ferron quickly responded with a diplomatic, "The news clip was far too revealing. I'll meet with Bohlm first. We're old university pals from South Eastern. Then again, Dallas was also a student there too." Lornae then doubled up and decided, "I'll fly down with you tomorrow, Milt."

In another corner of the globe, at Mei-Tan Contracting, both Mr. Shungmei and Mr. Tano were parties to one of those military build-ups. For their part they had met with Gunthar recently to secure a procurement of engineered to specification components for one of their aerospace assembly plants. Gunthar was smiling, as he was aiding in an arms race, where clearly there would never be a victor, as he pitted everyone against everyone - it was a chess game to him.

Back at the meeting, many emotions flared, from embarrassment to anger, particularly from the Chiu, Vilmajev and Gonsev camps regarding the allegations from the news story and from Mr. Dallas, who put them all on the defensive. At one point, Gonsev in his signature accent diplomatically lashed out with, "We all have a strong business and personal ethos, Mr. Dallas! GN-MG will focus on our core industries only. Engineering and consulting for customized components. New advanced manufacturing facilities and investments will all be within the Bagerville area."

A few applauses were heard again, including a few smiles from Chiu and Vilmajev, while Jason only rolled his eyes again and yelled out, "Not everything, and not everyone is for sale. Many here still have a soul and a conscience." Ruddy silent at the back, was sipping on a can of pop, scribbled down more notes. Under his note pad, he tapped his cell phone, to continue secretly recording most of the discussions in the meeting.

Gonsev this time became a tad uncomfortable with the accusations flying, so he decisively responded back, "Mr. Dallas, you insult me and look down at me, as if I were lowest common denominator. I have never wronged you. I have been recently wronged. As you may have heard, recently one of our main systems was hacked by an unknown intruder too. A serious breach affecting many in this room. However, I always believed in doing the most honourable things in life. From serving my country in time of need, to educating myself and building a future. I always did what was right and just. Yet, I also defended my interests, by all means necessary. Sadly, only memories remain of my wife and daughter, while certain scars never fade. But I have never wronged no one!"

This caused Jason to pause for a moment, before brushing it off, and turn his head, while many in the room were in awe and made no comments. At that point, Sula quickly stood up from his seat, raising his voice and outstretching his hands, "Now hold Jason, there is no need to dress down anyone here, by making such brash accusations and assumptions."

All dignitaries in attendance gave Jason a glance up and down, while diplomatically trying to avoid a war of profane words. Jason looked back and simply added, "Was there ever a rule of 72 for investing in this scenario? Yes Milt, asides from being a geologist, I also have a degree in economics. Remember? I also went to South Eastern. Both my parents were academics there too." That got the minister Ferron to simply want to wrap things up quickly, as he began dialling some colleagues from his cabinet to inform them that the meeting was over. Within the squabble unfolding, Lornae sent a quick text message from the corner of the room to minister Ferron, it read, "Avoid any incident. We don't need negative press now." Some of the media representatives in attendance were having a field fest scribbling and recording everything, as the drama unfolding contained some interesting news bits.

Sula for a second time tried to allay fears and muzzle Jason with, "That's enough Professor Dallas." At this juncture, Jason got a very cold feeling trickle along his back, suspecting that not only was the government involved, but so too were other individuals in this room. Dallas decried the lack of transparency, and then shouted, "Our nation's feckless leader - Lornae, has installed a stewardship, where his surrogates and stooges adhere to flawed regulations, legislation and myths under the tutelage of a questionable budget."

At that point, Jason, looking up at one of the bookshelves in the meeting room, took down a familiar leather bound book, read quite often, or at least on the seventh day, by a billion and half adherents globally. He opened it up, flipping through the pages, until he got to - Matthew 26, verse 15 - before he placed a ruler under the verse in the middle of the table. The entire room became quiet.

CHAPTER 14
Q90

In the distance of the industrial quarter of Q90, some vats were cooling off hot thick steel sheets, from the foundry and melting furnaces, while in another area, some water jets sprayed and lubricated some custom components. Away from the foundries, manufacturing plants, complex and warehouses nearby, where some vary precious resources within the mines spread out over a few kilometres, all within the Bagerville regions higher elevations. Illuminating the massive and sprawling complexes were large industrial lights, and the moon in its autumn evening setting in the horizon.

In the background, radio transmissions could be heard, and faint traces of voices and music from some workstations. Forklifts parked beside crates and skids, resting on warehouse floors, while trailers were parked in their docks bays for their morning runs to the airport and rail yards.

During the day, big wheeled excavators, boring machines and cranes were thumping, digging and drilling in the Q90, forcing dust, soot and particles to rise into the atmosphere and horizon, which darkened the skies below, in the lower elevations of Bagerville. Everyday the miners went in during the early hours and left in the late hours, coated in grunge of all colours, from head to toe.

Hundreds of hard hats and steel toe work boots toiled daily in the higher elevations at countless manufacturing complexes, factories and warehouses, getting their faces, necks and hands covered in sweat, dirt, grease, while producing incredible volumes of products for multiple industries globally. Nearby from one of the plants, a few welders were cutting some alloys outside, causing sparks and grinding noises, while another was creating flashes and zaps on a new steel beam, being designed for a domestic project. Various alloys expanded and contracted, while CNC lathes, electric discharge machines and intricate engraving devices placed their unique identities and marks on the diverse puzzle of parts. In the many plants, machines and people were micro-cutting, filing and measuring all the technical specifications, from ultra thin to wide shapes and everything in between.

Many officials, except for Jason Dallas, who always stood up for Bagerville, mysteriously silenced environmental concerns and complaints of pollution in the Soma River, which snaked and coiled around the Q90-area.

Professor and geologist, Jason Dallas hypothesized in some Bagerville Observer interviews, "Within the higher elevations, there exists some evidence of past, major volcanic activity, coupled with multiple meteor crashes that occurred thousands of year ago. As a result, there is a major contrast, the lower area is fertile near the Soma, while in the higher realms there are vastly diverse mineral and base metal deposits." At one point, about two years ago, there was a major ecological and environmental panic near Q90, when the Soma turned red for a few days. Jason came out to inspect the site, with various government and local officials. Some burst pipe that may have contained industrial sludge or ore, from one of the mines, caused the panic. Jason took numerous photos, which he archived at home, and sent a few tubes of samples to a former colleague at an overseas institution to get an analysis and perspective from another source. Within a few months after a report came out, new safeguards were put in place and stronger legislation was requested, to alleviate future concerns.

It seemed the moment important speeches were spoken, the Bagerville's Mayor Joe Bohlm came out of the woodwork from his cottage again, before disappearing again, after the last photo was taken. The rest of the mayoral duties rested with support staff at his office, who politely did all that they could, and answered everything relevant. Anything beyond the call of duty, which most mayors should do for the people, was relayed by either a phone call or an email. After the incident at the Soma River, and subsequent measures taken, professor Dallas took steps to inform Bohlm that, "Good governance is about consensus and consultation, before decision making. You were elected, as a result of our voices in Bagerville." By doing so, his words hit a note, that in the future, a collaborative approach must be made before any decision in Bagerville is implemented.

For Jason Dallas, one of his visits over a year ago at the ViGnChi R&D plant, was like having salt thrown on another wound. He was asked to partake in a research assignment with some international and ViGnChi scientists, when Vilmajev and Gunthar stood before the doors opened, holding out a confidentiality agreement that was to be signed, before any work was to begin. Jason looked at the document and stated emphatically, "You guys got to be kidding." Both Vilmajev and Gunthar just looked at him and said, "Not before, and not after." Many were already inside with lab coats on doing tests on some samples from Q90 under microscopes and computers. Jason reluctantly signed it, knowing full well, that what was to happen inside, would remain inside, and was never to be revealed. In the end, after Jason partook in the research and analysis of some classified work at the R&D plant, he refused to accept any payments from ViGnChi, telling them, "Everything I did today was for Bagerville. Only my professional opinions should matter, not my personal, which is diametrically opposed right now. Consider this work Pro bono publico." After that day, Jason was never the same with anyone from ViGnChi, and his distaste for their work in Bagerville and Q90, became even more critical, and unforgiving in every respect. There were many questions as to what was so secretive behind those doors, many speculations pointed to - the tension and durability of certain alloys, and their relation to stress factors and detection to various light, sound, radar and scanning sources - but to this day there are still no firm answers.

Since the split, engineers from ViChi continued with their day-to-day operations, while the defence and aerospace divisions were to be restructured slowly. Some were to join GN-MG, in new capacities, in either the consulting or engineering departments, that were be reorganized.

GN-MG, by virtue of the initial contract with the government, was entitled to a third of mines.

Gonsev made the trek up to the higher elevations multiple times weekly. This time he put on his hardhat and steel-toe shoes, and ventured towards the Palladium, Titanium and Tungsten mines. The Q90-area stretched over a radius of about two kilometres, where the mines and the veins led into the various deposits, sometimes hundreds of feet underneath the ground. Enormous equipment were set up everywhere near the mines, which were pulling out the raw ores from underneath the ground on conveyor belt excavating machines to the surface. From there, they were pushed onto swivelling chutes, and awaiting trucks that hauled the ores to process. Gonsev took numerous notes, samples and pictures, before preparing to head to the new GN-MG manufacturing facility nearby, that was being fitted with new robotic technology.

On his way to his car, he kept looking at a few samples of the Titanium and Tungsten in his hand, and then made a quick call to Al at the office to run a few questions through. Gonsev quickly dialled the number, "Al, I want to check the tensile strength of a couple of products, to ensure they withstand a few numbers. I need to verify, If the ultimate strength MPa for Tungsten is over the 600, and for the Titanium MPa is at least 300." For some reason for the past few hours the digits 600 and 300 were on his mind, so before heading to the robotic manufacturing division, he wanted those numbers. "Mr. Gonsev, let me do a quick test for you, and get back to you shortly," came a response from the other end. Gonsev after exchanging a few other questions and ideas, hoped into his car and waited a few minutes to get the confirmation, as now three words - stress, strain and tolerance - were gnawing at him. Within a few minutes his cell rang again, it was Al, "The numbers are correct, maybe off by a hair line. But in line. The other projects on the mastercam lathes are also still pending approval." Gonsev focused fully on the projects, and stated, "I'll stop by the offices within the next few hours to double-check the schematics again."

After the call, he went back up for a second trek by the mines, before finally heading back to the robotic manufacturing division, which took him about less than ten minutes to arrive at. He arrived in the parking lot and headed to the offices, where he met with some staff and one of the engineers, and stated, "You guys are great. The final test work on the articulating arms and delta robots in the plant is already done?" He then pointed to another area of the plant and continued, "Just some more wiring in some areas of the plant in that corner is needed, where some more cutting-edge machines need to find a home." Precision parts and components needed intricacy and detail, for many unique products they were now making with the detailed designs and models their clients needed. The work with all layers, geometric dimensions and symbols was now going to be far more cleaner and sharper, making all contours truly above any competitors ability.

About a hundred metres from him in the plant he noticed a few electricians near a wall still adding a few more outlet sockets to a work area, while nearby another was on a ladder wearing his safety suspenders and web tool belt, adjusting some lights. Gonsev was impressed and continued inspecting the plant for another twenty minutes, and came to a conclusion, "This new plant will be fully operational by tomorrow at this pace."

After the facility visit, Gonsev, was now going to head back to the new headquarters, to fire off a few emails and return a few calls, before finishing up some documents for an engineering presentation, scheduled for later with Gunthar and some clients.

Some clients had just flown in to Bagerville for some meetings with the new GN-MG, hoping to initial and secure a procurement of some highly sought after components and instruments, fashioned from some of the earth's greatest alloys.

Thomar Gunthar was wise and educated in many facets of life; he knew how to project power, and how to win any deal. About an hour after Gonsev left the site, Gunthar, arrived with his clients, to take them on a tour of Q90, and showcase the resources and new facility, where most of the fabrication and manufacturing would be done to their specifications. Gunthar gripping his handheld two-way radio in one hand and his hardhat in the other, his eyes scanned the horizon of mounds, open pits, surface mines and the enormous amount of heavy equipment, noise and people toiling. As he further scanned the horizon, he looked at the higher elevations above, and the lower elevations of Bagerville central below. He then quietly muttered under his breath, "I am the Pharaoh, and the messianic figure here and below. I am the master builder, while also the divider and conqueror. I am the giver and the taker. This is my game."

As his focus shifted back to his surroundings, he smiled, as he explained to his clients about the logistics, and the excellent rail and air links, and how their finished goods would be shipped to their respective destinations in a timely manner.

The clients were all amazed at the massive complex comprised of mines, facilities and the immense infrastructure everywhere. Gunthar looked at all them, while they were preparing to head back to the offices of GN-MG, and knew in his heart they were all on board.

Now smiling and enjoying the moment, Gunthar reiterated to them, "We will diligently manufacture to your specifications. You can coordinate everything with our engineering department, which is run by Mr. Gonsev. He will assist you in all technical matters. For payments, we prefer a - Letter of Credit - as it's more secure for everyone. We'll do that with our respective financial institutions, so that way the documentation and currency methodology can be done correctly. For further documentation, regarding exporting documentation, we'll do that with our fine folks in customs here in Bagerville. They'll take care of us. But even that doesn't matter, what matters is that we provide you with the highest quality products. Once again, I want to thank all of you for joining me up here, and now lets head back to the offices."

CHAPTER 15
GN-MG HQ

A few days later, Gonsev glanced at his screen twice, checking some details before proceeding to make a few calls to the engineering department. After analyzing the specifications for the components, he realized, "Once assembled this could be used for purposes other than what was originally detailed within the project." He did a quick conference call with his team, "I need all of you to halt work on this new defence contractor project, until I receive further clarifications and details. The specs are very questionable." All within the team listened, and gave him an oath that all work would halt until he gave them the green light. The 3D rendering began to resemble a very frightening image within Gonsev's mind. The rendering was like an illustration, of something that could be used for many wrong reasons, if in the hands of wrong people anywhere.

After the chat, he quickly called Gunthar, who was out of town at the moment, on a video link, to double-check things with him. He quickly typed in Gunthar's address on the video-link, and got through to him. "Thomar, I have some bad news. This new defence project, at the robotics division is very disturbing," Gonsev began. "Run it through, its a big contract, " Gunthar fired back, as he lowered his eyebrows, while trying to reassure him on the project, and questionable specifications. Gonsev without hesitation responded, "I cannot sign off on this project!"

It was a defence contract, and the crystal clear parametric models Gonsev was staring at, crossed a red-line, "These designs require some parts to be very durable, while others intricate and tensile. It's also detailing a need for composites to absorb detection and reflection. The angles need to be flat and sharp, which will reduce and redirect anything that comes into contact with it. These designs are disturbing. This is not something we should be doing for a low-key contractor." Gonsev quickly began to realize this was something larger. The design illustration contained the need for some stealth-like capabilities. The fact this project requested radar absorbent materials, and some composites really set the alarm bells off, and the puzzle began to form clearer into a very frightening aesthetic image.

Nearly a month ago at a very large military exercise near the Yellow Sea, the sound of jets roaring, streaking and screeching across clear skies could be heard. Criss-crossing, ascending, descending and mimicking scrambling jets and dogfights were showcased for many high ranking officials in dark green and camouflage fatigues, recognized by various stripes and badges, while others were adorned in smart conservative suits and sunglasses, who watched through binoculars in jeeps. Many foreign tongues, some unrecognizable were heard, though the central theme from a general and president was, "There is a need to achieve results, at any cost. We need our new jets to have highly advanced specifications made from some of the worlds greatest resources, that are capable of avoiding detection."

In the background were four aging jets that were parked near a few idle tanks and jeeps, by the control tower along a stretch of unused asphalt tarmac and runway. Beside them were a few rectangular buildings fashioned from steel, cinder blocks and bricks, where a few foreign camera crews and people in suits and green fatigues stood watching.

Both Shungmei and Tano, from Mei-Tan Contracting, were invited to the event, in hopes of assisting this valuable international customer, procure and then assemble stealthy and technologically advanced components for a new fleet of jets, that would aid in building and strengthening a rival powers political, economic and military position on the world stage. Shungmei and Tano reaffirmed to both the General and President, "We will be tendering a new bid for a government military procurement, along with a detailed proposal. We will make our nation once again prouder, and stronger than ever before."

Back at GN-MG, Gonsev quickly researched the company and noticed they were a not an approved company on their list of companies they dealt with, and then muttered, "Mei-Tan - these guys have a quite the reputation. Judging by the notes on the screen that Gunthar left, he inked this one deal recently after they passed through for a one-day tour, after a major trade show overseas." Upon confirming it was in fact a questionable contractor, and that this project could potentially get resold again to a rogue element, he got worried. Gonsev was familiar with some of those elements, and knew this project reeked, and the modus operandi was wrong.

It was not the first time that questionable contracts were shipped, the latest were the two trucks, sent in opposite directions to some overseas assembly plants. All this was arranged for and signed off by Gunthar. Not for the love of money, but for the love of power.

Andreas Wilfstig, was known in many global circles as a brash, middle-aged industrialist, whose tentacles reached into many precision instrument markets, as well as some shady arms markets in rogue states. His empire was primarily built on designing, assembling and distributing: custom surgical instruments, kitchen utensils and dual use military and civilian instruments. Wilstig operated under the moniker - Einzigartige Instrumente - based in an Alpine nation, where he was known as leader for a fine taste in all things expensive. Wilfstig had met with Gunthar a month ago at a convention, where the two agreed to meet again in Bagerville.

Wilfstig before leaving the convention approached Gunthar and told him, "I look forward to meeting with you very soon in Bagerville, to negotiate a mutually beneficial deal."

Within a week after the convention, Wilfstig made a short one-day flight to Bagerville to deliver the designs for some custom work and arrange for a payment in person, to avoid massive amounts of documentation floating through unwanted radar screens. Gunthar took him on a trip through various mines and manufacturing sites, and even quickly introduced him to Gonsev, who was at the time too busy to realize, that yet another questionable procurement was made. Wilfstig had some important customers awaiting the delivery, which he had to add some other fine layers at his assembly plant, so when Gunthar called him recently with the port and container number, his anxiety was reduced.

Back on the video-link, Gunthar began to exude his alpha male arrogance, as he peeled his darker personality off further, when he lashed back at Gonsev with, "I can build anything out of anything at Q90. Import or export documents don't mean anything. We can make anything for any customer. I have immunity. We have immunity. We can bypass everything and still do so from the legal point of view. Some chastise us, yet others know that we are in the throne of power, as we conquered, not by war, but by buying everything with money, and legally. We didn't write the rules of the game, Lornae altered it for us. Remember that my friend!"

Gonsev listened carefully and calmly responded back, "There are some laws that are still sacrosanct. There are voices within us all that guide us to choose from what is right, and what is wrong. This is wrong. I have fought on many fronts, but always for the right reasons. I have lost two people that meant the world to me, as a result of some peoples desires to conquer those that were on their native soil for centuries. I fought against this in the past, and will continue to do so in the future. There is a huge difference between - defensive and offensive. This I cannot sign off on."

At this point, for nearly twenty minutes a heated exchange of words followed, which boiled to the point of near disintegration, before Gonsev under pressure acquiesced stating, "Alright, I'll run it through Thomar, for the sake of the depth, scope and the jobs at stake." Within a few minutes during this melee of sorts, Gonsev felt disgusted, questioning everything around him and regretting having given taken some documents over to Gunthar's house once. He also remembered Vilmajev's trusted words and now regretted everything. He slowly loosened his half Windsor-knot tie, which was now half stained with sweat. He was very uncomfortable now, as his cuffs, collar and back of shirt were also damp. At the end of their conversation on the video-link, there was still a storm brewing in the air and the passions were still really angry and hostile. Running through Gonsev's mind right now was a need to head back to his old homeland for perhaps a lengthy visit.

After their chat, Gunthar did not feel entirely reassured and began to question Gonsev's loyalty and partnership, so he decided to embark on a visit to Gonsev's office to reassure him once more. Gunthar was at Bohlm's cottage, which he knew pretty well, considering he gave it to him on a platter for fealty. He went to Bohlm's and directly asked him, "I need some new permits for a project. How quick can you get them stamped?" Bohlm looked at him and said, "Everything is doable. I'll let you know the price tag by tomorrow." After receiving his confirmation, Gunthar cut his visit there short, but before leaving he made another call to a close associate, "Some events may change in the coming days, be prepared to meet soon. I may need your assistance once again."

After making the call, Gunthar like a dark serpent slowly slithered away from his nest to his car in a shadowy mist, while bringing with him an intricate device, that had many thin and round shiny contours which were made of some of the finest materials, loaded with six presents. On his way to the offices, Gunthar was still seething with anger, and had one hand on the intricate device, while the other on the steering. His emotions began to teeter between anger and rage, as he gripped the steering wheel, while shouting obscenities that only the inside of his car, and the netherworld could only hear. He was looking forward to a face-to-face chat with Gonsev now.

Before finalizing the signoff, Gonsev's conscience got to him, making him go back on his word, and he simply signed, "I cannot sign off on this," in a scribble that resembled a signature. The haunting images of his wife and daughter kept flashing before his eyes, questioning his motives, final outcomes and at what price. The project he scribbled on, passed to fabrication and the advanced manufacturing unit began work on the project within a few minutes. Gunthar's last words kept pounding in Gonsev's head, "The world is not what it appears to be. Always keep your friends close and your enemies even closer."

An ominous feeling crept over Gonsev after hearing those words. He placed both his hands over his face, and slowly pressed his fingers against his eyebrows and then forced them gently downwards towards his chin, before letting out a toxic exhale from the tension from within his chest. Gonsev then quickly decided to inform, Al at the engineering division again, "Al, cease all operations on questionable engineered to specifications work, until I give a firm go ahead. There are some serious problems with the specs. I'll be out of town for a short time, and get back to you soon." Now Gonsev's thoughts were focused on an overseas destination for a visit, so he also made an auto reply message for his email inbox, that he was going to be away, and to leave messages with Al at the engineering offices. Gonsev then proceeded to quickly send a quick note to a cousin overseas, and to Vilmajev stating, "You were right along. I'll call you soon."

Within another two minutes, Gonsev in a calm and composed manner copied all the files from his desktop and folders onto a flash drive, before he logged out of his computer, grabbed his cell, sunglasses and car keys. He then quickly took his two passports: one red and one blue, from his desk and placed them in his left breast pocket of his jacket, before he started to head out the door towards his car, all the while dialling a number. Within a few more minutes he had already entered his car, and had booked the next flight out of Bagerville, heading for an overseas destination, north of the Black Sea within the hour. He sensed a nebula of chaos, confusion and danger brewing within the entire area, and decided it would be best to disappear for a personal leave for a few weeks, until the questionable storm clouds dissipated.

Neither Gonsev, nor Gunthar suspected, or would have even guessed that they were being watched and listened to. Matt Dallas, hacked into their systems, and had copies of everything already, from the engineering conference call to the highly informative video link chat, that revealed a lot.

Matt couldn't believe what he was seeing and hearing, not to mention what was in his possession. He had evidence, in the form of audio, video and a trail of documents that could potentially bring about the arrest of certain individuals. He too also knew that the means he obtained the evidence was questionable, so he had to conceal his identity, if he was to bring this to justice.

He quickly constructed a folder with all the evidence inside and fired it off to Sheriff Ruddy and Vlad under an alias to avoid being detected. There were to be many surprises awaiting those who opened their email accounts soon, enough to bring about a great story or two.

CHAPTER 16
WHO, WHAT, WHERE, WHY, WHEN?

Arriving home, Vlad wasted not time after a lengthy chat with family members to request some quiet time, as he was gonna go up to his room and try to lay down, or do some work on his computer. As he sat down, he began to reflect on all the events - Bagerville Polytechnic, the cornfields and waking up at the hospital. The five Ws wouldn't leave his mind: Who, What, Where, Why and When?

He tried to shift focus, as he looked around in his room, but couldn't get the five Ws out of his head. After a few minutes, he tried to focus on his closet, his clothes on the floor, and the papers strewn everywhere on his desk. He made no physical effort, but mentally attempted to calm himself down, before his anxiety was heightened again from the sounds of passing traffic from his bedroom window. He tried to brush off the uneasy feeling, thinking those feelings were quite normal after the ordeal he had gone through in the past few days.

He finally got up and did a big stretch, and then sat down again, before deciding to log into his computer, when he noticed a Bagerville news item come up. News broke on the internet first, and then on TV, that the two who were responsible for their violent rough up, were apprehended earlier in the day in Bagerville, after a tip off from an anonymous source. Sensing the need to eliminate a problem that had been festering now, Gunthar advised an associate, "We need to wash our hands, and cut the umbilical cord of the two liabilities, as too many eyes, ears and mouths are searching for answers." A tip off from an unknown witness, framed the two individuals responsible for the rough up, thus sealing the deal for their apprehension.

The two yet to be named individuals, apparently were concerned about their jobs, after all the noise with the ViGnChi split, and the rumblings from various sources that Jason and his protesters were out to get Q90 investigated, and closed down. Furthering to the complication, was info that the two had followed Vlad at The Sundial and overheard some of the details, which infuriated them. They were also part-time students at Bagerville Polytechnic, and had also overheard Jason Dallas on many times rail on all activities, vowing to have the place looked into. They were immediately suspended, and possibly on the verge of expulsion from the Polytechnic by Richard Sula, who said, "The outcome of the investigation and any possible trial will determine any further steps to be taken."

Within minutes, Vlad's cell was ringing, and within less than five minutes multiple messages were left on his voice mail from: Sheriff Ruddy, Professor Jason Dallas and Matt. Shouts could also be heard from downstairs from Vlad's parents about the news just broadcast on the TV. Vlad was not only floored, but also speechless for a few minutes. Shortly after, Matt gave him another ring and told him, "Make sure to check your email, there maybe a present waiting for you." Vlad tried to brush it off as a joke of some kind, "Yeah, sure Matt. What present?"

Once again Matt, sticking to his message repeated, "There is a present waiting for you. In fact, there is a gold mine waiting for you inside. Use it wisely."

After they had got off the phone, he logged into his email account to check. Someone, under an anonymous name had sent him a folder, which inside contained a plethora of audio, video and document files. As he opened a few of them, his eyes widened as he viewed the text and images and video clips. He then quickly closed the files, before standing up on edge, to see if anything was watching him. His suspicions and earlier dabbling into research on the ViGnChi work seems to have been correct - there was something very wrong with the whole deal.

At this point, an idea popped in Vlad's mind, so he grabbed his car keys and jacket, then ran down the stairs telling everyone, "I'm stepping out for a breather, be back soon." With every breath and step taken, a vivid picture of the ideal story was brewing within the confines of his creative imagination. Something far more telling, than the one he thought he had uncovered. This anonymous email was a gift from the gods, as it reconfirmed everything. He was on the verge of the story of the decade.

He quickly jumped into his car, while his dad, Rob Voss, followed his moves through the living room window and said to his wife, "I'm worried that things are getting way out of hand in Bagerville lately. At least we still have this house left, and the greatest son Vlad. They can never take that away from us." Vlad drove with determination to the offices of The Bagerville Observer to pitch a story to the editor. Arriving about 10 minutes later, happy to see the editor, who was working on a news piece. He asked him, "Can I get a few minutes, to pitch a story to you?" The editor sat in his chair twisting and turning while intuitively listening to Vlad, before he gave him the go ahead, and a promise, "If the story is good, you'll have a gig on a full-time and salaried basis before graduation."

After the go ahead, Vlad with his USB flash drive in pocket, headed for the resource library in town to begin some quiet work and further research. When he arrived, he spent a few hours digging through some microfiche documents, before opening up his computer and logging into his email account again. As he opened his inbox, he noticed Tim sent him a few files. Some shady financial files. The numbers seemed to have been fudged by some account representatives within GN-MG. Vlad couldn't believe his eyes, so he stood up for a moment to clear his mind. He then looked through the big open window leading to the parking lot and the Bagerville Mall, thinking and formulating a storyline.

Earlier in the day, Tim while doing some information technology related analysis work, at one of the larger banks in town stumbled across some files. Tim was part of a team implementing a new platform for the international trade-financing department, when he noticed one interesting file before his eyes, "What do we have here. It seems we have an interesting file under the banner GN-MG and Mei-Tan Contracting." Immediately and conveniently he copied the file to his flash drive without anyone noticing anything, then during his break he quickly sent a message and attachment to his friend Vlad, and a copy to Matt.

Vlad was busy online doing some research, reading and working on his story, when he noticed his inbox chirping with new mail that just arrived. He noticed the email with attachments was from Tim, "Awesome. Look's like Tim sent me something."

Vlad opened up the email and file attachment and took a few minutes to digest the contents contained with, "Wow. This contract looks pretty interesting and it looks like someone high up altered it too. The components. This looks like a procurement for a nation to rebuild its arsenal."

Vlad continued to go through each line of the financial document, along with the notes contained within, at least a few times thinking to himself, "This material is very disturbing, considering it was altered to avoid problems when leaving the country." Further, he realized to what extent Tim went through to retrieve this file, "This file could land quite a few people in major hot water. Tim must have dug this out of a hidden cave."

When Vlad finished with the financial file, he checked his surroundings again, didn't see anything strange, so he saved the files on his USB flash drive. Vlad then continued to sift through other files, while turning down the volume, then watching, listening and reading. The contents were equally explosive, if not worse. His initial words were, "Unbelievable. Absolute corruption." He quickly looked around him, thinking he spoke too loud, before he continued smiling and whispering to himself, "This is one story that will shake the foundations of many quarters of the globe, not just Bagerville."

As his last word ended, the pristine silence of the library was disturbed again, this time by his cell, so he peeked at the incoming number, turning down the volume further, after realizing it was Matt. Before he answered, the line cut. Then a text shot across his screen, "I hope you like your present," from Matt. He got a chuckle and then began to work on a very interesting narrative for the story.

CHAPTER 17
RESEARCHING FOR THE TRUTH

For days Sheriff Ruddy Sark would rarely leave the confines of the division, only taking urgent calls, the rest he asked others to deal with. There was a lot of clatter, chatter and phone ringing in the background. He closed his door, only to go to the washroom, grab a quick bite to eat, or grab a can of pop. He literally had his sleeves rolled up at his desk, with countless documents scattered. Manila file folders, printouts and even long form government issued documents, all laid out one on top of each other in a collage of papers that needed to be examined thoroughly for any hints of evidence.

Outside his office an officer was working on a case, and typing some documents on an old typewriter, whose tapping was echoing through the entire office. Ruddy noticing the irritability went to close his door firmer, placing an old rag near the opening to block the sound.

The division's dispatcher just smirked, before getting up from her seat for a moment to go to the water cooler, and grab a few folders from a file cabinet. Outside the windows the three police cars were parked, one of them had left their high beams on, before an officer noticed and walked over to shut them off.

Observing many of these activities at the division, through one eye and one ear, while trying to focus on his research, Ruddy shook his head and took a deep breath, before muttering, "Another hour to go, and there is still way too much distraction here."

He then glanced at his phone and listened to the recordings he did at Bagerville Polytechnic. He parsed through Vilmajev, Chiu and Gonsev's words a few times. He thought about Jason and tossing the book down at the end. He thought about that moment and then said, "It's as if it were a reflection, guiding someone through a metaphor, or about being sold out for small change." He dwelled on that moment and pondered that maybe there actually may be something far deeper in those words, "Perhaps thirty pieces of whatever currency may have been more than a betrayal to the nation."

He began to flashback at Bagerville Polytechnic again, this time when two individuals roughed up, Jason. Those two individuals were just apprehended. He heard the radio transmission and saw the news clip flash on the TV screen at the station. The two were to be taken in to a holding cell, in another part of town, on various charges based on an anonymous tip. The newscaster orated a story about the two's intentions were stifling Vlad and Jason's efforts to undermine the Q90 work, where apparently the two were employed part-time at one of the facilities. The two were terminated immediately.

Further, they were also part-time students at the Bagerville Polytechnic, though now Sula, decided to suspend them. Ruddy took a deep breath and told himself, "There's something in this and it's probably deeper." He was sure this case would last a year or two in courts. Again he thought about it, and asked himself, "No links to ViChi or GN-MG?" Something again told him, "Dig deeper, Ruddy. There are various charges. The case could last years."

At this point, he decided to pack it in and head home, and possibly do some work later. He headed out the door with all his items and into his car, firing up the ignition and having a million things race through his head. While driving he decided to alter his path home, by stopping for some gas and groceries at the plaza. He passed by The Sundial and waved to Frank, letting him know, "I'll pop in for a beer another time. Gotta head into Bagerville Foods for some items." Within minutes, his conscience began to bug him in the parking lot, so before heading into Bagerville Foods, he took a longer walk over to The Sundial. As he entered he saw Frank there smiling and began, "You got a minute?"

Frank just dropped everything and moved closer to him, giving him a firm handshake, before countering, "Always for an old friend and brother. What's up?"

Looking around for the nearest seat in a quiet spot, Ruddy motioned Frank to sit down, "Grab a seat pal. Frank, me, you, Bohlm and Dallas used to do this at least once a month. Get together at least once a month, as old friends, shoot the breeze, have a drink. We'd be honest with each other, regardless of what we do in our professional lives. I'm not going to preach our Bagerville mantra, but when things go in directions beyond the scope of what is right and what is wrong, things need to be addressed. Regardless, I must maintain a deep professional attitude, while adhering to the rule of law, and at the same time try to be impartial. But it all doesn't stitch together fully."

Frank shook his head and continued listening, before ordering a few drinks from one of his staff, and asking, "What things Ruddy?"

Ruddy stretched his chest out, before putting both his hands on the table, leaning over closer to Frank and quietly whispering, "The whole structure in Bagerville. I can't pin it down yet. But our dear friend Bohlm may be a part of something."

Frank gave Ruddy a sarcastic look and asked, "Bohlm? What? What are you saying Ruddy, that our mayor, and brother is doing something? Today, I have The Sundial. If I didn't, I'd still have - The Moltracheen Estates. Maybe Beth would still be alive today. But hey, a new road passes through my forefathers lands now." Frank was able to hold back his emotions, but Ruddy could see, and feel the pain he felt.

Ruddy then continued, "I'm almost positive. Bohlm, Q90, these entities and Lornae's team may have stitched together something. Follow the money some say. Still, I shouldn't be telling you this. Frank, keep a lid on things. Lets just talk about something else now."

Both sat together and chatted for another hour, before Ruddy got up, quickly finished his shopping and proceeded to go home to continue his work.

A few hours later, when he got home, he tossed his folders on his living room table, hung his keys on rack, and tossed his shoes off into a corner. He then proceeded to head to his bedroom, where he changed his clothes into something more comfy - sweat pants and a t-shirt. Now relaxed, he went back to the kitchen to grab a can of pop out of the fridge, and head into his living room, where he turned on the TV, before planting his now two-hundred pound plus weight into his couch. His thoughts started circling in multitudes of directions over everything, so he walked to the washroom and splashed some cold water in his face and stared at the mirror before him and said, "I can't pin it. I just doesn't make sense. The whole Q90 deal, and Bohlm seems to be flush with cash."

In his living room, a Bagerville news reporters story on the TV caught one of Ruddy's ears, "Sources close to many defence departments overseas tonight are indicating that Bagerville-based GN-MG, are possibly supplying some questionable regimes with highly advanced technological components, causing military build-ups in many regions." Ruddy listened attentively at the story, while making his way back to the living room area, where some of his work he brought home still lay in folders. After a few minutes he grabbed the TV controller near the coffee table, and lowered the volume, and then focused back to the folders on the table and his laptop. Once again, he took a big sip from his pop can, and then continued poring over documents, graphs and some videos on his computer, while in the back of is mind a cluster of the past few day's events and the news story were circling. On one of his walls was still an old framed picture from twenty-five years ago - of him, Jason, Frank, Joe and old Jim Dallas on a boat on beautiful summer day fishing on the Soma. He just smirked at the photo, before he keyed in a government web address, and dug up all information related to the Lornae administration and ViGnChi at the time. Specifically he was after all legal documents related to the deal of the century, though some were sealed under the secret banner and filed for safekeeping. He found a few interesting documents related to the ViGnChi deal, and then began to scour and pore through keywords that may hold some value in his dig for some answers. Over the course of a half hour he went through at least a dozen documents, all which were laced with legal jargon and business acumens indicating that things were done in accordance with the actual agreement.

After digging through the countless documents, he decided to log into his email account to check his mail. Upon opening his inbox he noticed an email from, Matt Dallas, which read, "Someone will be sending you some very interesting evidence shortly relating to work at GN-MG." Ruddy thought that was strange, especially after that news story just minutes ago, and wanted to dial Jason's house to check with him about that comment. He grabbed the phone, and called Jason quickly, "You got a minute Jay?"

"This has to be something. What's up?" Jason quickly responded knowing that Ruddy never called him late in the evening unless it was serious.

"I got a strange email from Matt. The gravity of it relates to Bohlm, Q90 and those entities," Ruddy calmly relayed his thoughts.

"Ruddy, I've been fighting this dog in our town since day one. From protests; being vocal in every corner of the globe I visit; all the way to my face-to-face encounters with all of them. You know my feelings, and I'm sure you and Frank share my sentiment to an extent as well. As for Bohlm, I fear he may have sold his soul. But that's just my thoughts, Ruddy. As for Matt, I'm sure he shares our sentiment too, and only wants the best for Bagerville. Whatever he sent you is most likely a result of some investigative work. You know what I mean? Nothing less. Same goes for Vlad and Tim. They have been vocal in every manner as well, while never breaking the law," Jason countered back.

Ruddy agreed to his friend's comments, before digging his heels further, "I know Jay. Since this autonomous atmosphere in Bagerville for Vilmajev, Chiu and Gunthar, it seems some, including Bohlm has buckled to every whim of these guys. I'm digging deep into this old friend, and I'm sure that sooner, rather than later, we'll all find out how this all ticks, and on who still has a conscience." Both chatted for about ten minutes regarding many possibilities, before Jason delved into another one of his metaphors before ending with, "Ruddy, you wear the badge, Bohlm only wears the title, while something within Q90 may be the canary in the coal mine."

Ruddy just let it blow over his shoulder, hung up the receiver and continued scanning his inbox mail, until he noticed another message this time from an anonymous address, which contained a folder. Inside were video clips, audio files and some other interesting documents.

Evidence of questionable government policies, corruption and possible sale of goods, not allowed to be exported without authorization. This went high up the food chain. At that point, he had a quick flashback to the hospital and Vlad, and all the documents he brought that were uncovered, yet then they didn't make sense. This was all fitting together very clearly to Ruddy, that in fact there may actually be - a canary in the coal mine - and that corruption runs from the top to the bottom.

Ruddy's eyes lit up, as he went through each file and document three times, before uttering some profanities. Looking down the list further, a sense of deep disgust began to fester in the bottom of his stomach, when he read that mayor Joe Bohlm might also be involved. This was now confirming to him his initial speculations. Ruddy thought about the cottage, exotic trips, cash and new pickup truck, and deep down knew in his heart, that a mayor with the salary he is given annually could never muster enough cash for such a lifestyle. He had known Joe for decades, and it was difficult to digest the evidence, which he had to deal with. He was grappling with immense corruption on a scale that was so large that it defied logic.

Once again, Ruddy looked at the phone again, grabbed it and wanted to call Joe, who was once again was at his cottage not aware of many events that had happened in town lately. He then slammed the receiver down, as thoughts of betrayal of public trust, taking bribes and silence to corruption were racing through his head. It was a difficult moral and ethical dilemma that was facing him now that the mayor must be brought down too, for crimes that no citizen of Bagerville, or even old friend, could stand behind.

He made a final and difficult decision and headed back to the police division and consult with some other department heads, before he was going to issue an arrest warrant himself for the mayor's arrest, which he wanted to do himself.

CHAPTER 18
THE FINAL ACT OF REDEMPTION

Well planned and executed, Matt felt at peace that he had uncovered and exposed many corrupt and deceptive tactics in Bagerville, a source of revulsion for his father, Jason Dallas. He had put together a folder containing many audio, video and document files and forwarded them to Vlad, and over to Sheriff Ruddy. Further, Tim also was at task at a local financial institution, helping uncover some very interesting files, which were also made available to Vlad. Tim grabbed his cell from his cargo pants pocket, as he walked down a corridor to a quieter spot, and quickly dialled Matt's number, "I found a tonne of more files here. I'm gonna put together a folder, after I finish scanning a few more documents. Check your email and let Vlad know that more goods will be on his plate soon. I'm sure true justice will reward our efforts soon. This is for my family, Bagerville and everyone that was taken advantage of." On the other end, Matt listened and confirmed to him, "The time is definitely nigh. This will finally get exposed soon."

For many months now, Matt closely examined and analysed every operation related to the Q90 area and Bagerville, in a hue of silence, while formulating a detailed plan on how to capture evidence necessary to facilitate change. He made sure that he left no traces, so as to remain anonymous, though many knew that it was Matt, behind the scenes uncovering the curtains to one of the final acts.

The rough up of his father and Vlad was temporarily solved, though he suspected that more hidden hands were involved, which managed to silence their tracks. Matt Dallas remembered their two faces from The Sundial, they were sitting at the back. They did look familiar, as they had indeed crossed paths at Bagerville Polytechnic and some pub-crawls on a few occasions. Little did he know, they kept listening and looking over towards their table the whole time, where Matt, Vlad and Tim were seated, drinking and chatting, all the while planning a terrible plan. Some people could be bought for very little, while others would wither in poverty before selling their souls to the lowest bidders.

After uncovering the plethora of files that Matt sent, under the guise of anonymity, Vlad was quick and determined to reveal the story to Bagerville and the world. Tim's documents sent also very detailed and revealing, and without them, the puzzle surely would have appeared far more bias, skewed and highly speculative. It took him less than twenty-four hours to stitch together an amazing timeline and narrative.

His major news story, which first broke in, The Bagerville Observer the next day, also went viral online as - Bagerville: Corruption and illegal sales of prohibited goods by altered documentation with government blessing. Vlad's story, ended up being a five-page exposé - including quotes, images of high-ranking officials and actual sections from altered legal documents that were uncovered.

The nation's government in Ophidia was reeling after the release of the story. The opposition parties heckled the Lornae-led government at the next day parliament sitting. Shouts of, "Shame. Sell-out. Corruption. You lied to us," were heard in the chambers and halls of the parliament. Lornae and his party sensed their impending demise was coming. The speaker of the parliament attempted to quell the unrest and anger from the opposition, and his calls for "Order. Order," were drowned out and ignored, as the shouts became louder than the tapping of the ceremonial gavel.

The friction boiling over in parliament was broadcast live to the nation, and all in Bagerville watched including Jason and Gordana, who were sitting in their living room when it all began to boil over. Jason had earlier been in the garage tidying up some rock samples on shelves and cabinets he had set up, from past digs, excavations and research assignments. Gordana came in and said, "Jason, you should come in and check out the news. Lornae and his party are arguing with the opposition live. Its ugly. There is also some major story that just cracked somewhere from here in Bagerville, about deep seated corruption. It's gone global." Jason paused, took a deep breath, quickly pushed a wood cabinet to a corner with two heaves, and then responded, "I'll be there in two seconds. I want to check this out."

Based on Vlad's exposé, and subsequent behind the scenes in-depth coverage, the editor of The Bagerville Observer, amazed at the stories and publicity generated, immediately offered Vlad a full-time position, with a substantial wage increase and autonomy to cover stories globally.

As the stories began to catch the headlines internationally, everything began to unfold with momentum. When Ruddy stitched his evidence into a crystal clear and coherent picture, it only confirmed his initial speculations of the narrative, so he got on the horn with everyone he could muster, beginning with the nations defence department. Steadfast and determined he sat down, and began to dial the number, all the while preparing a folder on his laptop ready to send to all the relevant authorities.

The line rang twice, before a female voice answered, "Defence department, how may I take your call." Ruddy calmly began, "This is Sheriff Ruddy Sark of Division 01 in Bagerville, patch me through to the command centre." The female voice quickly responded that she would patch him through directly to Defence Minister, General William Vysten. Once Vysten picked up the receiver, Ruddy continued, "General, this is Sheriff Ruddy Sark from Bagerville, I have some startling revelations that may shake the foundations of this nation. I've uncovered a large amount files relating to: bribes, corruption and cover-ups with the Lornae administration and the special economic zone here in Bagerville." Vysten listened, while with his left hand he began to tap his pen on his desk, before asking, "Sheriff Sark, do you have any evidence to substantiate your claim?" Sark confidently replied back, "Yes I do, General Vysten. I have just sent a folder worth of files to your department, through a secure server to your email address. Please take a look." General Vysten continued his conversation with Ruddy for another four minutes, while checking the files sent, before telling Ruddy to stay on the line. Vysten sat in his chair and peered over to his three stars on both shoulders of his shirt, and took a deep breath, before he began dialling - Supreme Judge Peter Bollxop - to once again enact the Crisis Measures Protocol and request warrants. Within seconds, the other telephone line began ringing, and after the third ring, Vysten began, "Judge Bollxop, this is General Vysten. We have a mess down in Bagerville. Apparently there is evidence-indicating Lornae and some others are in collusion with some individuals in the special economic zone in Bagerville. It seems bribery, corruption and possibly fraud is rife, while there is some evidence of major customs tampering with falsified documentations as well. I ask, that you enact the Crisis Measures Protocol and issue a blanket of warrants for the Lornae administration. The government and constitution must be suspended and a change of guard, until we have new elections." Bollxop just listened and replied, "Here we go again General Vysten, and it was just over three years ago that we had the last crisis. I told Lornae, that I would be cautiously optimistic and monitor all of his legal and regulatory changes. He was warned that if any element crossed a line, there would be issues to deal with on the legal front. General Vysten, I will enact the Crisis Measures Protocol and have your warrants sent to your office with the next twenty minutes. You take over for now. Lornae must be notified, and he must address the nation immediately to acknowledge the change of guard, as to reduce any economic, political or social unrest that could ensue. After that you may arrest him, if need be." After the call with Bollxop, he got back to Sheriff Sark and advised him, "The Crisis Measures Protocol will be enacted soon. You may need to deal with some local issues soon with your Mayor down there soon." Within a very short time frame, General Vysten, also dispatched the armed services to alert them of the situation. This was his second time allowing for the armed forces to quell a situation. This time, Vysten's decision to seek those powers, were mostly political and not economic. Vysten was swift, ordering an immediate response to a crisis unfolding. It took him minutes, as opposed to days that it would take some officials, to ensure this situation was dealt with all the resources available.

Within an hour, multiple police and defence forces were executing search, seizure and arrests in many corners of the country. Flashes of white, blue, green, yellow and red lights and sirens, coming from many vehicles, could be heard throughout Bagerville and around many government buildings in Ophidia. The military gauntlet of power asserted its supreme control of all functions of the nation quickly. General Vysten in liaison with the Supreme Judge Bollxop quickly suspended the powers of the parliament for 24 hours. General Vysten continued with his duties, and quickly informed President Lornae that the military, the Supreme Judge Peter Bollxop and the ministers would assume control of the country until, "All investigations into corruption and criminal activities were complete."

Within minutes, sensing national security was at risk, President John E. Lornae prepared a hastily prepared speech to deliver, inviting all medias that were within the parliament to cover it, as action needed to be taken. His address to the nation was quick, "Based on the serious allegations brought forward, some of which have implicated many levels of power, I have decided that it would be in the best interests of nation to resign effective immediately, and temporarily pass all presidential powers to General William Vysten, Supreme Judge Peter Bollxop and the ministers, until such time as new elections are held."

Upon finishing his speech, Lornae attempted to quickly head to his address, which was only minutes from the parliament, and grab some belongings, planning to flee to an unknown destination until things quelled down. Yet as he arrived at his address, there were military police awaiting him with a warrant for: breach of trust, embezzlement and corruption related charges. The cuffs were slowly placed on his wrists, while his rights were read to him, at which time he was advised to seek counsel immediately from a lawyer. Lornae remained calm and quiet, while only stating, "I have done nothing wrong. I have always looked after the best interests of the nation."

Further, within another ten minutes the entire government was brought down, as another four cabinet ministers were indicted on corruption. The power centre was now entrusted in the supreme court of the country, which quickly decided to hold new elections within weeks. Immediately, the major global bourse exchanges began to see volatile spikes in commodity indexes and prices, as a result of the uncertainty and negative sentiment which was unfolding.

There were multiple arrests also made at GN-MG, where some staff were clearly and deeply immersed with the design and goods that contravened many legal parameters. Further, various contractors in different global territories were brought to heal, as were two customs and border officials, who were taken in on corruption and altered documentation charges. They actively allowed for many highly questionable goods to enter and exit Bagerville, many times turning a blind eye for a sealed envelope.

Thomar Gunthar was immediately taken in on many bribery, falsification of document charges and weapons related charges to name but a few, from his residential home. He heard the loud voices and sirens, and did not make a fuss as he opened the door and only grabbed his jacket and shoes, before laughing and raising his hands, reminding those who were arresting him, "I will sue for justice, and with vengeance."

The other GN-MG magnate, Gonsev was nowhere to be found. Searches were underway everywhere, yet the only traces found were an international flight out of Bagerville on a one way ticket. An international arrest warrant was issued for Mikhael Igor Gonsev, for possible document falsification and criminal dealings at GN-MG. Gonsev was nowhere to be found. Rumours were spreading that Gonsev was overseas, yet he mysteriously vanished within thin air. Many speculated that he sought refuge in another neighbouring country, were he had complete immunity, and was shielded by powerful forces within the highest echelons in a large Eurasian nation.

Near the end of the arrests, Bagerville's Mayor Bohlm was forced to resign on some lesser charges of corruption, as Sheriff Ruddy didn't have the heart to arrest or charge him, provided he immediately resign and retire from public service. When Ruddy approached Bohlm's residence in Bagerville, the message was crystal clear, when Joe Bohlm asked him, "Are you here to arrest me old friend?" Ruddy just paused, shook his head, and looked Joe Bohlm straight in the eye's as he held a document which he passed to him, before declaring, "Please resign." It was a painful moment for Ruddy, but in his heart he knew it was the right thing to do, for Bagerville and for the many affected by the wide-scale damage by the stench of deceit and corruption. Ruddy also thought for a moment about the Voss, Zelk and the Moltracheen families and their lands, that were wrongfully expropriated. It was personal to him. Frank was a close friend, just like Jason Dallas, and just like Joe Bohlm once was. Mayor Bohlm just stood there looking at Ruddy, and the document for about half a minute in silence, thinking that he was going to be arrested.

Ruddy did not flinch, he just stood there looking at Joe, a person he had known for a very long time, then once again made a request, "For the sake of Bagerville. For the sake of the nation. For the sake of your own good, please sign this document and resign now. Go wherever you want, but never return to Bagerville in any capacity asides from being a private citizen." The message was bold and effective, as Bohlm sensed the seriousness of the document, and immediately signed it without a second thought, before saying a few last words to Ruddy, "I'll pack a few items and I'll be out of here within an hour." Ruddy just stood there and nodded his head, without saying a word, before he turned around and headed back to his car with the signed resignation.

For now, within Bagerville and the rest of the nation, the defence forces were once again in many corners, this time to assume control, and assist in installing temporary institutions, to be run mainly by groups made up of citizens and other strata of society with legal and economic backgrounds. These groups were now tasked with restoring many constitutional and democratic values; open up all the secretive documents, and head to the courts to amend certain decisions that may have been made under duress, and influence of monetary reward. The arrests were so abundant in every corner of the country, that they not only became an international embarrassment, but a spectacle.

There was very little alarm, and no arrests at the ViChi camp, as all their work and documents were found to be in order. All activities would continue as is, or as Chiu and Vilmajev promised, "For the entire duration of the contract signed with Lornae." As for GN-MG operations, most of their operations were asked to be continued under a court-appointed board of directors, set up for a thirty day period, until further information and instructions were to be given, as to the status of the assets and the employees. ViChi stood up to the plate immediately offering to reabsorb all assets and employees, as they argued the contract was still legally binding.

During the entire melee, Matt rejoiced at the sense of accomplishment and justice, and while driving home beside the Soma. He smiled while cranking up his radio dial, as he passed the higher elevations, through a main road past The Sundial in town, before continuing his journey home. He kept smiling as he passed by a few apple orchards and a winery, where he saw a few ladders beside fences and a few bushels full of autumn harvest blue grapes. A sense of accomplishment had hit him now in his heart and mind, and he knew deep down inside he had in a way vindicated his father's journey to expose the dark curse Bagerville was living under. The shell of corruption was now bursting wide-open, exposing all those who enslaved the residents to a grey mist of false hope and prosperity. The truth of the deceitful fortunes, exploitation, lies and cover-up by all levels of power was now flooding all the media streams globally.

When he approached his home, parked the jeep on the driveway, he decided to slowly walk through the front door this time. As he entered the through the door, he was greeted by his mother, who had dinner all set up and was watching all the breaking news on the TV, with a million questions to ask.

An unbelievable past few days produced not only drama and excitement, but also major changes everywhere. Bagerville was once again set to transform, as the sweeping stories became a reality once the legal system began to work again to the benefit, rather than the detriment of the town and nation.

Upstairs Jason Dallas heard him come in the door. Jason was reading some topographic maps and examining some charts for a new article. He was asked to write for - Geologia Scientia - an international geology journal that published articles monthly on vast topics from exploration, research, analysis and news. He began to write down a few notes, but quickly got distracted by all the events that unfolded recently, that he began tapping his hand lens with his right index finger. Once again he looked at his hand lens, and remembered some very dark cave explorations and some sedimentary basins he used it in to examine various rocks and even the soil. It was almost like a second pair of eyes for him, letting his mind delve deeper into the finite world of every granule, texture and contour. Jason's eyes now shifted to one of the old posters still in his study, one that meant a lot to him from the nostalgic point of view, The Bagerville Harvest Fair. He smiled at it, while reminiscing his long gone grandpa Jim, and said, "I will bring you back one day. I promise."

As the footsteps and door shut downstairs, Jason wrapped up his work and this time, with a deep breath he took the lanyard and hand lens off his neck and placed it around his Petrographic microscope on his desk, before slowly getting up and began his walk downstairs with a bright and invigorated look in him. Justice was served not only with the fools that roughed him up, but with the arrest of Gunthar too. He felt somewhat vindicated and yet empty, as if the albatross around his neck was freed. Jason now pondered on the conversations he had with Matt in the past few days regarding all the events in Bagerville, and what future would look like, before shrugging it off and saying, "Tomorrow is another day."

Nonetheless, he greeted them both, Matt and Gordana affectionately with warm embraces, before they had an amazing roast beef dinner with salad, and lots of cold drinks. They spent the entire evening together reminiscing and sharing stories of the past and present, until Jason looked at both Gordana and Matt and said, "The time for a sabbatical is now."

Printed in Canada